Storm Between the Stars

Book 1 of The Fall of the Censor

Karl K. Gallagher

D1065869

© 2020 Karl K. Gallagher.
All Rights Reserved.

This is a work of fiction. Names, characters, businesses, places, events and incidents are either the products of the author's imagination or used in a fictitious manner. Any resemblance to actual persons, living or dead, or actual events is purely coincidental.

Published by Kelt Haven Press, Saginaw, TX.

Cover art and design by Stephanie G. Folse of Augusta Scarlet, LLC: www.scarlettebooks.com.
Editing by Laura Gallagher.
3D spaceship model and interior art by Winchell Chung

To those actually building rockets to take us to the stars.

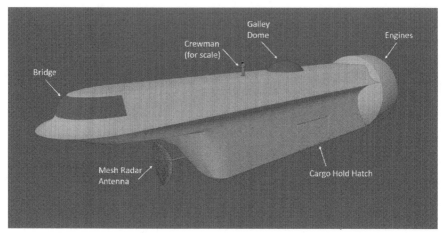

Merchant Ship *Azure Tarn*

Storm Between the Stars

"All stations report readiness for survey," ordered Captain Niko
Landry.

"Navigation, sightings and inertial coordinates agree to seven
digits."

"Power, ready for surge."

The rest of the bridge crew made their reports. "Proceed with
survey pulse," Landry said.

The power and sensor techs went down the checklist as they
prepared to shunt maximum power to the radar dish.

Landry listened with half his attention while he watched the clouds
of hyperspace through the bridge windows. To his eyes the near-zero
density formations looked the same as the solid ones. It took a radar
pulse to see which his ship could fly through and which would smash
her to bits.

"Bringing full power on line—now!" said Welly, the power tech.

On previous survey points this had triggered whines and creaks
from overstressed machinery. This time the bridge lights went out.
Along with the artificial gravity.

Emergency lights came on, drowned out by the glow of
hyperspace. Buckles clicked as lazy crew hastily fastened their belts.

Captain Landry silently counted to ten as he watched his feet drift
up from the deck. When the power tech still hadn't said anything he
prompted, "Welly?"

"Working it, Skipper. Generator is down, we're running on

batteries."

Batteries were obviously working since all the bridge consoles still functioned. Landry started counting again.

"Circuit breakers aren't tripped. The generator was producing power up to ninety percent of max. Then it went to zero."

"Right. I'll go aft and check on that." Landry unbuckled from his seat. "First mate, you have the con."

"Aye-aye, Captain," said Lane Landry from the Comm station. Having his wife as first mate was a good way to run a family-owned ship. Keeping their interactions formal on duty was a good way to reassure the crew they were staying professional.

Once he closed the bridge hatch Landry arrowed down the corridor faster than he'd tolerate any of the crew going. If the artificial gravity came back on he'd be in danger of a broken wrist or worse. But he suspected there wasn't much danger of that happening without warning.

Landry could hear shouting through the closed engine room hatch. He sighed and flung it open.

"—was one job you could do without me watching you! Just pour in the lube, check the dipstick, done!" Gander kept bellowing as his apprentice tried to get a word in to defend himself. The clang of the hatch didn't stop him either. "You gotta get the details right!"

Landry broke in. "Chief!"

Gander muttered, "Keep your mouth shut," at the apprentice then turned around. "Yes, Captain?"

His tone was neutral. The chief engineer was properly deferential elsewhere in the ship. In this compartment he considered himself in charge.

Captain Landry let it slide. "What's with the generator?"

"Fumbles here"—a thumb indicated the apprentice—"only gave the generator half the lubricant it needed. It seized up."

"I didn't know there was a second lube tank!" burst out young Tets.

"Keep yer mouth shut in front of the captain! We gotta dismount it and replace some bearings. Should take an hour or three."

"Very well. Get started. The sooner we finish the survey the sooner we'll be home again. Need any more hands to speed it up?"

"No, we've got it." Gander turned to the generator housing. "Gimme a three-quarters."

Tets flew across the compartment to the wrench rack. He grabbed the right one as he bounced off the bulkhead, putting it right into Gander's palm.

Landry watched them work. Tets watched closely, bagging each bolt as Gander popped it out. *I guess monkey-see, monkey-do will serve as training. It'll have to unless Gander learns to explain things.*

He decided to go back through the cargo hold to see if anything had come loose with the gravity out.

The emergency lights left the hold full of shadows. Two flashlights darted among the stacked crates like fireflies.

One popped into the open. "Hi, Dad!"

Glare.

"I mean, good afternoon, Captain." Marcus Landry flushed, visible even under the emergency lights.

"Afternoon. What're you doing?"

Marcus' assistant cargo handler popped up. She had the sense to not shine her light in his eyes. "Just checking the tie-downs, sir. Making sure nothing's loose in free-fall."

"And Alys suggested more practice in zero-g maneuvering," added Marcus.

The captain translated that as playing tag to sneak in some grab-ass. But they didn't have much else to do right now. "Don't let me interfere with the inspection."

"Yessir," they chorused. This time they took diverging paths through the maze.

Landry drifted along the ceiling of the hold. The cargo was an eclectic mix of machinery, toys, and luxury goods. When a hauling job had fallen through he'd sunk most of his savings into buying speculative goods for a run to Svalbard. Then this survey gig popped up and he'd grabbed it. So instead of collecting hundreds of marks in interest his savings were gathering dust in the hold.

The survey charter is buying me some time, Captain Landry thought, *but I need to find a way to make some real money or the payments on the ship will eat me alive. When we get back to civilization I need to find a speculative venture we can take on.*

Well, if the survey took too long they'd have to make a resupply stop on Svalbard or Iolite. He could sell the junk then. "Silver linings everywhere," he muttered.

The forward ladder took him back to the bridge. "Power generator's under repair," he announced. "Everyone take a break. Be back in ninety minutes."

***

Gander's voice rang over the PA. "Generator back on line. Power in one minute."

Landry thumbed the intercom button on his chair. "Thank you, chief."

It was a bit over a minute when the lights came back on. A few moments later his feet dropped to the deck.

Welly sighed and put away the bag she'd been holding open.

Hums and whirs indicated more equipment coming on line. Red indicators on consoles turned green.

"Run basic diagnostics," ordered Landry. "Let's make sure the power drop didn't break anything."

The only problem found was an auxiliary navigation processor needing a reboot. Landry concealed a smile. No problems would leave the crew grumbling about wasted time. One problem was perfect.

With the ship back in running order they repeated the survey routine. This time nothing interrupted. The overhead lights flickered as the sensor dish fired a pulse of radio waves into hyperspace.

The sensor tech's console lit up as returning echoes created an image of the shoals.

Hyperspace was full of clouds. Some were wisps that a ship could fly through without slowing. Others were shoals. A ship striking one would be as wrecked as if it ran into solid rock.

Eyeballing clouds couldn't tell the difference. You could fly a ship through empty space without radar but you'd always run into a cloud before reaching another star. Wisps and shoals looked the same. Color, glow, shadows, flickering lightning all appeared in both.

Surveys were critical for maintaining the safety of shipping lanes. An ordinary freighter didn't have the radar power to spot a shifting shoal in its path. High-traffic zones had dedicated survey cutters checking for intrusions.

Zero-traffic zones, such as the wall enclosing the Fieran Bubble, could be left to tramp freighters with oversized military surplus radars. It wasn't quite charity work. The walls had to be checked every few years in case a shoal started moving toward inhabited regions. But it wasn't urgent. Their homeworld had been trapped in the Bubble for centuries, cut off from the rest of the human race by a solid sphere of shoals. The fear was that they'd close in and leave the three worlds in the Bubble only able to reach each other through years-long trips in normal space.

"Welly, did you have a power drop out during the scan?" demanded Betty, the sensor tech.

"Huh? No, it was a clean draw."

"It's not a clean scan. Looks like the radar didn't transmit for the middle third."

Welly just shrugged.

Captain Landry broke in before Betty could ramp up the argument. "Run the scan again. Watch your power throughput."

"Yes, sir."

Betty repeated the scan. The radar swept the bow quadrant from port to starboard. "Okay, power's steady. But look at that."

Captain Landry unfastened his seat belt and took two steps to stand behind her. The center display on the sensor console compared the radar returns to the plot of the last survey mission five years ago.

Most of it showed small displacements, the typical amount they'd seen in the past three weeks of survey work. The center had a roughly triangular zone with no return at all.

"Looks like a cove formed," said Landry.

"Deep enough to have no return at all?"

The navigator had the data echoed on her screen. "There was already a dimple in the wall there. It's been five years since the last survey of this stretch. Plenty of time for big changes."

"I didn't ask you, Soon," retorted Betty.

The captain raised his hand to avert another argument. "We'll go in and look for the bottom. Helm, ahead slow. Sensors, do a short range full sphere scan. Let me know if you see any visible movement." Landry returned to his chair. If there was any sign of the cove closing up again he'd reverse course at full speed.

Betty and Roger responded, "Aye-aye."

Roger steered them down the centerline of the cove. Wisps of fog obscured the view. He relied on radar data and suggestions from Soon.

An empty patch let them see the walls of the cove. It was a boring bit of hyperspace. The walls were smooth, like a pale orange stratus cloud folded into a prism.

"I'm detecting motion, sir," said Betty.

Landry sat up straight. "Where?"

She pointed out the port window. "That wall is receding just barely enough to measure."

"I like receding," said Roger. He kept the ship aimed down the centerline.

A cloud waited for them. Radar said it was just a wisp so they entered. Lightning flickered off to starboard, too far away to affect them.

"Whoa!" Betty fiddled with her displays. "The shoals just widened out."

Roger's hand tensed on the throttle lever. "Safe to proceed?"

"Yeah, plenty of room."

They broke out of the wisp into the clear.

Everyone was silent as they stared out.

They could see farther than they ever had before. Glowing cloud banks marked where stars might lay in normal space. A dark thunderhead might indicate a black hole, if the theories the academy taught were true. More clouds cast shadows, changing the pastel blues and pinks and yellows to deeper colors.

"Are we . . . out of the Bubble?" asked Roger.

Captain Landry replied, "Yes. Helm, all stop."

"All stop, aye."

Then there was more silence.

A streak of lightning leapt from the dark thunderhead. It zigzagged through an arch of pale purple cumulus then lit the edge of a green horsetail before grounding out in the puffy mounds surrounding a sun.

The far side of the volume was indistinct. Clouds of all varieties overlapped. Glows were too faint to tell their cause from here.

Some clouds were drifting. Probably wisps. Shoals moved slowly if at all.

There were no ships close enough to see.

"Comm, are you picking up any traffic?"

"Nothing digital," answered Lane Landry. "The high energy signals I've listened to have all been stellar noise."

"Right. Sensors, make a spherical scan."

Betty and Roger worked together to rotate the ship between each radar pulse. It took twelve shots to cover the sky.

"Sir, the hole we came out of is in a rough wall. Other than that, there's nothing close enough to give us a return."

"Thank you."

Captain Landry picked up his mike and pressed the PA button. "All hands, crew meeting in the galley."

Azure Tarn's galley had a clear geodesic dome over it. The sales copy for the ship described it as an attraction for passengers. Landry considered it another sign the designers couldn't make up their mind what they wanted the ship to be.

The bridge crew were slow to tear themselves away from the view. The mechanics and cargo handlers were already there when they arrived.

Gander stood with his head tilted back, glaring at the new suns. Tets lay on the floor wearing a broad smile. Marcus and Alys slouched in chairs to look out the dome.

She was leaning toward him, Landry noted with no change in his expression. *That's a complication I don't need.*

The bridge crew found seats and resumed staring.

Several minutes went by.

"How long has it been?" asked Alys.

Marcus answered, "Over nine hundred years."

"Nine hundred and fifty-seven," corrected Soon. "Francis University is planning a commemoration for the one thousandth anniversary of Arrival."

"We can rejoin the human race." Alys' voice had a dreamy tone.

"If any of them survived," rasped Gander. "It was a hell of a war our ancestors fled. Might have killed everyone. Did your textbook have the picture of the last evacuation ship? The half ship the Gap closed on?"

"Yes," said Lane calmly. "We all saw that. But there's been wars in the Bubble and we survived."

"We can't be sure anyone else survived the Great War," said Gander.

"Could be a good opportunity for us if they didn't," said his apprentice from the floor. "Imagine what's lying in the ruins to be picked up."

Marcus laughed. "Guarded by mutant monsters?"

"This isn't one of your fantasy games," said Captain Landry. "If we find a depopulated planet we're not landing on it. I want no part of any war plagues."

Betty started. "We're not going to go back and report, sir?"

"I haven't decided yet."

"We can't go back!" Tets pushed himself up to sitting. "This is our chance to be famous. The first people to recontact the rest of humanity—or prove they're gone—we'd be remembered forever."

"Fame doesn't pay the bills. But there ought to be chances for profit there. Our cargo is discount ware at home but it'll be exotic out there." Landry waved at the dome.

"Or technology has advanced so far they'll consider it trash," said his wife, wearing her first mate hat now.

"That's one of the risks, yes."

Alys hadn't taken her eyes off the dome. "If they advanced far enough they could have transcended. Not be humans any more, but gods."

"Ha!" Roger laughed. "That's ridiculous. Our technology has been advancing. They can't be that far ahead of us."

Lane Landry kept her voice gentle. "Our advances are rediscovering what was lost. The Evacuation Fleet didn't have enough people to maintain their technology base. What progress we did make was interrupted by wars and the horrid flare. We're barely ahead of what the Evacuation fled from."

"If they're that far ahead we can sell our stuff to historians," said Soon.

"Good thought," said the captain. "How long would it take us to get to the nearest stars?"

"I don't know," she answered. "I don't have a distance. But if we run along the wall for a day I'll have enough parallax to make an estimate."

"Good."

Betty burst out, "Wait! If we go exploring aren't we violating our contract?"

The first mate held up a tablet. "The contract requires us to fully measure all deviations from the previous survey. So technically we need to survey all that before we're done." She waved at the cloudscape.

"I think they'll forgive that lack of compliance," said the captain with a chuckle. "Let's start on that parallax run. Survey shifts are over. We're back on watch rotation.

Gander made a face. Landry wasn't sympathetic. *If he'd hired a second mechanic like I told him to he wouldn't have to work twelve hour shifts.*

***

A day later parallax revealed that one of the dimmer stars was only a week's cruise away. *Azure Tarn* set out for it.

Most of the crew was looking forward to seeing what they'd find.

Betty needed a talking to from the first mate before she'd shut up about death traps and contract violations. Gander grumbled as well but he was always complaining about something, so Landry didn't fret over it.

The cheerful ones still had some worries. Roger and Soon ran simulated evasive maneuvers to prepare for a hostile welcome. Marcus and Alys rigged disposable coveralls for the spacesuits to prevent any contaminated dirt coming on board.

The first mate found the captain reinventorying the cargo. No crew were there to see so she slipped an arm around his waist and leaned into him. "Talk to me?"

"The condiments are our best bet. Exotic and a novelty. The other foods will just be novelties. The rest are iffy. The tractor parts we as might as well drop out the hatch when we get to normal space."

"Don't throw away anything if you don't have to. We could sell the parts to historians."

That brought a chuckle out of her husband.

"Now come to bed. You're not working, you're brooding."

He didn't move, other than looking around to see if any of the crew had snuck in. "I'd rather brood over trading possibilities than whether we're headed into a war or a graveyard or some realm where they've learned to make ships disappear by saying a magic word."

"So you've thought through each of those and made a plan?"

"More or less."

"Then let's go write those plans down."

An hour in their oversized cabin left them with a series of flowcharts. Most branches ended in 'run like hell' or 'beg for mercy.' A few went to 'make a deal.' They were the likeliest branches.

"There," said Lane Landry. "Feel more in control of the situation?"

"No. More in control of me."

"That's enough. Roll onto your belly, Niko."

A back rub soon put the captain to sleep.

The first mate checked with the bridge before turning in herself. Roger reported hyperspace was still empty.

"Okay. Wake us if anything happens," she said.

***

Roger's voice crackled on the PA. "Captain to the bridge. Captain to the bridge."

Landry dropped his fork on the galley table and raced through the hatch. The first mate followed more slowly. Marcus had been enjoying dinner with his parents. He rummaged in the cabinets to find two covers to put over their plates.

"What happened?" demanded Landry as he burst through the bridge hatch. They were in open interstellar space. There shouldn't be *anything* happening.

Roger stood up from the command chair and pointed out one of the wide viewports. "We saw something, sir. Can't figure out what the heck it is."

His finger indicated a glowing, swirling mass which hadn't been there during Landry's last shift. It changed as the captain watched. Puffs of yellow disappeared under purple which was replaced by green. His wife let out a low whistle as she came up next to him.

"It has a radar signature," said Soon. Her display bore a blurry black-and-grey version of the sight. "A weak one. It's not a shoal."

"No, it's not. It's a storm. Congratulations. You two are the first Fierans to see a hyperspace storm since . . . well, ever. We can't have storms in the Bubble. Not enough room for one to develop."

Landry only recognized it because he'd taken classes beyond what was needed for his Master's Warrant to command a ship. He unpacked rusty memories to explain the sight to his bridge crew.

Hyperspace was not a vacuum. It was filled with aether, part liquid, part gas, and part nightmare of physicists. *Azure Tarn* could coast through normal space, but in hyperspace she needed to keep thrusting or drag would bring her to a stop. The ship's maximum speed was governed by the strength of her hull to stand up to the aether pressure.

Even in the Fieran Bubble there were "waves" in hyperspace as the aether was pushed by stellar flares or shifting shoals. The pressure difference wasn't enough to damage a ship, as long as it wasn't moving at its top speed.

In the wide open galaxy supernovas or fast moving black holes would smash the aether like an explosion. The waves would bend around shoals and stars, dispersed in some directions and concentrated in others. This storm looked like a wave had been focused straight toward them.

"Can it hurt us?" asked Roger.

"Probably," said Landry. "There's records of storms that crushed ships to dust. We'll transition back to normal space as soon as we feel a shiver."

Both spacers looked relieved. He felt indignant at that. How crazy did they think he was? Landry looked back at his first mate, leaning on the back of the command chair, for reassurance. Her smirk wasn't reassuring.

"Watch our heading more closely. The bow wave of this might push us off course. And track its position. If we're lucky it'll miss us."

Nine hours later it was clear they would not be missed. The storm filled half the sky. Pressure sensors on the hull reported increasing force on the port side. Landry readied the ship for transition.

He visited the engine room to check on Gander's preparations. The hyperspace twister was shining. He hoped it was in as good shape on the inside.

"We're all set, Captain," said Gander.

"Thanks, Chief. My real worry is when we go back to hyperspace. If we come out too close to the storm, how fast can you turn around the twister to get us back to normal?"

Military ships could do an in-and-out in less than five minutes— but *Azure Tarn* didn't have the fancy gear they did. Nor was Gander certified to military standards.

"Mmmm." The chief engineer twisted a polishing rag in his hands as he thought. "Could do it in ten minutes from when you give the word. But that's going to put some wear on it."

"We can live with that. Prep for a switch back as soon as we go through, just in case."

"Aye-aye."

A whistle sounded around them. Tets looked up from the bearing he was cleaning. "What's that noise?"

Gander chuckled. "It's the storm, lad. And it'll get louder until we drop out."

Back at the bridge the first mate reported, "I took us down to half ahead thrust. The density keeps going up."

"Right." Landry put his hand against the bulkhead. There was just a faint shiver as the storm beat at the ship. They didn't need to jump yet . . . but if they were slowing down there wasn't much point to staying in hyperspace. "Take us back to normal space."

"Aye-aye." Lane Landry turned back to the bridge crew. A few commands brought the ship through the stomach-twisting transition to normal space.

Once everyone recovered Landry ordered, "Sensors, let's get a scan for junk around here."

A few minutes later Betty reported, "Nothing. Not even dust."

Well, they were many light-years from the nearest star. This would be as empty as space got.

The next twenty four hours were boring. The off-duty crew rotated through a continuous card game in the galley. When it was time to go back to hyperspace everyone was in place early.

"Initiate transition," ordered Landry. He'd have to eyeball the conditions before deciding whether to stay in hyperspace.

The "twister" created a bubble in hyperspace which the ship fell into. Once transition was complete the hyperspace generator dropped its field. In a normal transition someone with a sensitive microphone pressed to the hull could pick up the slap of the surrounding aether collapsing the vacuum of the bubble.

Everyone heard the slap this time. Bright light shone through the viewports on the bridge. Roger lifted his hand to shield his eyes. Then he grabbed his console with both hands as the ship rolled to starboard.

Captain Landry held to his chair with his hands and the footrest with both feet. The ship followed the roll with a nose-down pitch that nearly tossed him out of the chair. With his usual post-transition vertigo he could barely tell what was the ship and what was his unhappy brain.

Someone was throwing up. A light flashed outside the viewport, leaving purple spots in Landry's vision. Someone screamed. The bridge lights and half the displays went dark. A whiff of smoke cut across the smell of vomit. The roar was too loud to be an air leak—he'd feel the breeze. Must be aether on the hull.

He looked up. There was a crack in the viewport. Not enough for a leak—that'd be a high pitched hiss and there wasn't any of that in the noise on the bridge.

His fingers groped for the intercom buttons. "Gander, transition back!"

No response.

"Gander, transition back, acknowledge!"

The first mate stood up from the comm console. "Intercom's down. Circuit breaker. Most of them tripped after that lightning strike. I'll go tell him."

She staggered across the bridge, catching herself on the hatch coaming as the ship lurched again. Then she went through.

Her husband reached a hand toward her, wanting to do that himself—but they couldn't both leave the bridge.

The captain turned back to the bow. "Roger, apply thrust, take us down and starboard. Let's try to get in this current, see if that makes the ride easier."

"Aye-aye," gasped the helmsman, barely audible over the roar of aether outside.

Lane Landry didn't have much trouble passing through the corridor. With both arms outstretched she could have one on each bulkhead. That let her brace against each surge and lurch. She kept her feet all the way to the galley.

In the hatchway she hesitated. Going around the outer wall would take longer, and only help against surges from one direction. The middle was asking to be thrown across the compartment. But there was the table to hold on to . . . and it would be faster. The first mate lunged for the table.

She reached it before the next lurch, nearly losing her grip as the ship pitched down. Then there was a rattle louder than the roar of aether outside and a chair bounced off the table straight at her head. They were made to hook into the deck in case of free-fall. Someone had been careless last meal.

Lane ducked almost fast enough. One chair leg scraped over the top of her head, annoying but not as painful as her hands after absorbing a surge. She started moving along the table, pulling herself forward with the table edge and locked-down chairs, hoping she could make it out of the galley before that chair came flying back.

Then she was through the hatch and could brace herself in the narrow corridor again. The engine room hatch was open. She could hear voices and see a moving light.

"Hold the damned light steady, the jumper needs to plug into the capacitor just right."

That was Gander yelling at his apprentice again, just as if they were doing routine maintenance.

"There, the juice is flowing now. Check the brushes. They lose some wires every cycle."

The first mate slammed against the coaming of the engine room hatch with a grunt. A roll came at exactly the wrong moment. The noise made both chief and apprentice look up at her.

"Ma'am, you're bleeding!" cried apprentice Tets.

A swipe of her hand proved the moisture dribbling from her scalp was blood, not sweat. "It's not urgent. Orders from the bridge, transition to normal as soon as you can."

Gander grunted. "That's what we're working on. If you were coming to tell me to not jump, I'd have words."

The first mate didn't answer. Now that she'd delivered the message she had attention to spare for her head. Poking at the tear stung like hell, but she didn't think she had a concussion.

A deep moan cut through the aether roar. "What's that?" demanded Tets. Lane wondered the same.

"Hull ribs are starting to bend," said Gander. "We've turned to put the wind at our after quarter. The bitch isn't designed for that. Wants pressure on her nose."

The pitching and rolling subsided. The moans of the structure came and went.

"Topped off at last!" Gander shoved a lever home and the transition generator started whirring.

Then it froze as the energy was dumped into the generator field. Blessed silence and stillness fell on the ship. Lane heard ringing bells, but knew that was just the transition.

"Thank you, Chief," said Lane. She'd thank Tets for his part later, where Gander wouldn't hear.

The cut on the first mate's head was the worst injury. Everyone had at least some bruises. Inspections showed no major damage, though some electronics needed new components. Morale held up. As Marcus put it, "Now it really feels like we're on an adventure."

The captain waited forty-eight hours before trying hyperspace again. This time they were in the big empty. The storm was receding on the starboard bow, far enough away they could spot all the navigation markers they needed to resume their course.

***

Three days later they arrived at the shoals surrounding the star. Bright stripes in the cloud resolved into rifts allowing passage into the center. They picked one free of wisps and headed in, all crew on duty again.

"This is pretty," remarked Soon.

Landry agreed. The shoals on each side were layered in blue and pink. The starward shoal glowed brighter. The outer one reflected lights shining from around the curve of the rift.

With no charts Roger steered for the brightest light. Betty and Soon worked together to make a record of where they'd passed.

The navigator reported, "It looks like this rift follows a nautilus curve. Two loops should get us close enough to find a planet."

"If the rift doesn't pinch closed," muttered Betty.

It was only one and a half times around the sun when Welly pointed out the window. "Is that a gravity swirl?"

A patch of the inner wall twisted under the strain of some normal space object's gravitational pull.

"Good eye," said Soon. "It's not very wide. Rocky planet. Probable location off the port bow. Want to take a look, Skipper?"

"Yes, but not from this close," said Captain Landry. "Keep going another ten minutes so we're clear of any junk around it."

"Aye-aye."

Landry felt the tension on the bridge rise. In a few minutes they might contact the rest of the human race.

Soon watched the chronometer. "Ten minutes, sir."

"All stop."

"All stop, aye," said Roger.

The pastel clouds sliding by the viewport slowed as the aetheric resistance of hyperspace stole the ship's momentum. When they stopped Landry pressed the engine room intercom switch.

"Chief, are we ready to jump back to normal space?"

"Ready, aye. Capacitor fully charged, twister oiled and inspected." Gander sounded mildly irritated over having his readiness questioned. For him that was cheerful.

"We'll recharge the capacitor before going anywhere in normal. Stand ready."

"Aye-aye."

Landry switched to the PA. "All hands. We are returning to normal space. Jump in three, two, one, jump."

Gander hit his cue. The twister took a sphere of space into another universe. The glowing clouds blurred and became infinite black, spangled with bright points.

Landry held tight to the arms of his chair as his inner ear insisted gravity had gone sideways. When the urge to throw himself to the deck passed he said, "Report."

"Fine." "Okay." "Fine," said each of the bridge crew. Soon put her bag away.

The transition affected everyone differently. Landry knew one spacer who swore he could tell where they'd arrived by what he smelled during the jump.

"All hands report," Landry said over the PA.

"Engine room. All crew fine," said Gander.

Marcus' voice was next. "Cargo hold. Both crew fine."

"Sensors, do a short-range check." They'd come out clear of any star or planet, the signs of hyperspace hadn't lied to them. But any place in normal space could have a bit of gravel traveling fast enough to breach their hull.

"Nothing nearby, sir," reported Betty.

Landry began to relax. "Good. We'll charge up the capacitor then turn the radar loose on that planet. We're probably too far from the primary for it to have anything interesting. But we'll check."

The younger crew looked at the image of the world on the ship's camera and speculated what might be under the ice.

The first mate, sitting at the Comm station, began typing excitedly. "I'm picking up a radio signal. Digital code. Standard navigation message format. It's partially in English. 'Mining station Fwynwr Ystaen' and coordinates."

The message was forwarded to the other bridge consoles.

"The coordinates match the origin of the signal," declared Soon. "It's about two thirds of the way around the primary."

She worked with two displays, one showing the solar system they were in and the other an extrapolation of the hyperspace rift they'd been travelling through.

"We can get there twenty percent faster in normal space," she concluded.

"Good," said the captain. "But we'll go through hyper. I want to keep an escape route open."

The correspondence between normal and hyper varied enough that they couldn't follow the course of the rift in normal without a good recent survey. If they went through a volume matching a shoal and tried to enter hyperspace the ship would become a burst of metal fragments.

Once the ship was cruising between glowing clouds again Roger burst out, "They're alive!"

Nods went around the bridge.

"Don't be too excited," said Lane Landry. "It could be automatic."

"Automatics need maintenance. So there were people here at least a century ago." Roger kept steering *Azure Tarn* down the middle of the rift, but his gaze seemed to be past the clouds.

Soon continued updating her chart with the actual dimensions of the rift. "Okay, I don't see a swirl, but I think this is as close as we can get."

"Very good," said Captain Landry. He ran the crew through the ritual of transition again. This time Soon did throw up. Her stomach hadn't recovered from the previous two so close together.

"I have the mining station beacon again," said Lane, after she'd recovered from hallucinatory ringing bells.

"Hail them," said the captain.

Lane typed "FREE TRADER AZURE TARN REQUESTS PERMISSION TO APPROACH." A keystroke transmitted it on the same frequency as the beacon.

"How long until we get an answer?" asked Roger.

Lane shrugged. "Depends on if anyone's watching the radio. If everyone is asleep or working outside it could be hours. It's on repeat in case they're not recording."

"If we don't hear back soon we'll go to minimum manning." Landry hid a smile at their reactions. Normally they were happy to have some free time. Now nobody wanted to miss what might happen.

Only ten minutes passed before a reply arrived. The first mate read it out. "Welcome trader. Permission granted."

"Sounds like potential customers," said Landry. "Take us in, Roger."

Betty grumbled, "Or they're baiting a trap. Permission to ping the planet?"

"Denied. Blowing out spacesuit radios is a bad start to a relationship."

"They speak English," said Soon. "No having to do sign language. That's good news."

"New message. Audio transmission frequency." Lane turned on the bridge speakers. Background static hissed and crackled.

A stranger's voice spoke. "Oorru zpaim foozzer."

The crew traded glances. Everyone was equally confused.

"Oorru zpaim foozzer," repeated the stranger.

Lane spoke into her mike. "Greetings, this is *Azure Tarn*."

More gibberish came from the speaker. The tone of voice shifted from calm to confused.

"Does anyone there speak English?"

Gibberish again.

She put the mike down. "I'm going to send a query."

A flurry of keystrokes sent 'DOES ANYONE THERE SPEAK ENGLISH?' on the beacon frequency.

The speakers angrily burst out, "A ain zthaigim oomriz!"

"Oh," said Welly.

The power tech undid her seat belt, walked across the bridge, and picked up the mike. "Ooru mamam zpopon."

The next response was just as incomprehensible but much more cheerful. Welly answered in kind.

Lane unbuckled, stood, and waved Welly into the comm console seat.

Welly continued the conversation then paused to talk to the captain. "Sir, he's inviting us to land at his base, and he wants to know where we're from."

"We accept. And tell him Fiera."

He reflected on that. There was no harm in strangers learning the name of their homeworld. Being able to find it . . .

"Betty."

The sensor tech jerked out of her brooding. "Sir?"

"Can you rig something to trash all the navigation and sensor data from this trip on my command?"

"Easy. I'd have to bring the backup chips up from belowdecks."

"Do it."

Betty went out the hatch, muttering, "First sensible—" as it closed.

The conversation wrapped up with cheery equivalents of "See you soon."

"Welly. How the *hell* did you figure out their language?" demanded

Captain Landry.

Welly shrugged. "Once I recognized a few words it was obvious. They're speaking English. Just with a strong accent."

"That didn't sound like English."

"Pronunciations changed. 'P' became 'TH'. 'M' and 'N' moved closer to each other. 'R' has faded to a grace note. And the vowels all changed. It's a continuation of the Great Vowel Shift the language had about two thousand years ago. I, um, was an English major before I dropped out."

Landry looked around the bridge. No one else considered it obvious. "Good work, Welly. You'll come along to interpret."

Welly nodded, face flushed. She turned to the first mate and made a gentle wave to ask if they should change places again.

"I can handle power," said Lane. "You stay there in case they call again."

She paused in thought. "I wonder how their pronunciation drifted so far. We have recordings from Earth that came with the evacuation fleet, over a thousand years old. The speech is perfectly understandable. Don't these guys have that?"

"They might be some isolated backwater," offered Soon.

"*We're* an isolated backwater."

The hatch reopened. Betty came in holding a pair of memory chips in one hand and a package of explosive bolts in the other.

***

The planet was a rock. Impact craters dotted the surface. The rips of the mining engine made a bigger scar. Plumes of dust kicked up into the near vacuum drew the eye. The engines were larger than any freighter in the Fieran Bubble. Huge maws ingested rock, a mobile sorter processed it, and slag trailed behind.

Azure Tarn descended toward the base. It was a massive refinery with small living quarters attached to one side. Also on that side were two clear expanses of rock striped as landing pads. The ship had been directed to the yellow one.

Roger divided his attention among thruster power levels, short-range radar, the belly cameras, and the view out the windows. A smoothly curving descent would not stay clear of the refinery or the mountains of slag surrounding it. His course doglegged to avoid them.,

Quiet whispers from Soon warned when their course came too close to a slag pile or drifted off the landing pad.

In the captain's chair Niko Landry gripped the armrests. His palms itched to take the maneuvering controls. But he'd hired a helmsman because he didn't have a young man's reflexes any more.

Normally *Azure Tarn* landed at a shallow angle, letting the thrusters act along her centerline. The slag mountains forced them to come down almost vertically at the end.

Landry checked the system display. Yes, the landing gear were extended. Then a loud thump sounded, and a quiver palpable through the artificial gravity. The display turned the forward legs light blue. Two more thumps.

Roger sighed in relief. "Touchdown. Weight on gear."

"Good landing. Secure for in port," said Landry.

Lane responded, "Gravity off."

Suddenly they were all a third lighter.

"First mate, you have the con. Welly, let's go suit up."

As ordered, Marcus and Alys were donning space suits when the other two reached the hold. Landry made a brief speech as they dressed. "We're not going to do serious business here. Just a little deal, trade them some food or gadgets. What we really want is directions to the nearest inhabited world. And find out what we can about what things are like now.

"Don't give any information away for free. Watch your expression. If we all gasp at something they say they'll realize it was important and be more wary.

"Our story is we were updating a routine survey and found a new short cut. Hyperspace is twisty enough to make that plausible. Let them believe we're from an in-contact world if we can."

Naturally they had questions. After some discussion Marcus pointed out Welly could refer all questions to the captain and use translation difficulties to avoid answering the hard ones.

The forward personnel airlock was large enough to hold all four of them. The cargo handlers held pressurized sample cases, crowding them.

The outer door lowered to make a ramp.

As he walked out onto the planet Landry looked up at a slag pile and suppressed a flinch. The miners had taken advantage of the low gravity to pile it steeper. To Landry's experience on heavier worlds the mound looked ready to avalanche down to bury his ship and crew.

On the other side stacks of metal ingots rested between the landing pads and the refinery. Each stack was a slightly different color. Looked like the refinery separated out lots of different metals. The slag piles must be iron, silicon, aluminum, and similar junk common in any system.

Two spacesuited figures waited outside the building. One waved.

Hospitable of them, thought Landry. *Some places people sit inside and wait for you to figure out their damned never standardized airlock controls.*

Welly traded unintelligible pleasantries over the radio with them.

The airlock they went into was meant for vehicles. Two flatbed haulers were parked in it. Despite its size it repressurized in seconds once the door closed.

The hosts popped off their helmets.

Landry checked the readouts on his forearm. Pressure acceptable, oxygen fraction acceptable, temperature brisk but survivable. He took his helmet off. His crew followed.

The air stank of sweat and dust and scorched wiring. Not bad enough to be unhealthy. But enough to prove these people didn't care about more than meeting the minimum standards.

The locals were both men. Their skin was the color of a cookie ready to come out of the oven. Hair and beards were trimmed to a fingerwidth, too short to catch on their helmet ring.

A short corridor led to a lounge area. Couches and chairs faced a blank screen. Three tables with benches were beside a kitchen wall. Two men stood as they entered.

The room showed signs of a recent and cursory cleaning. Stains showed here and there. No trash remained.

Welly handled introductions as spacesuits were doffed. The boss miner was named Zahm. He was one of the pair who'd met them outside. All the miners had firm handshakes.

The men shared a round face and strong eyebrows. Landry wondered if this was a family business. Not unusual for a frontier operation.

"It's just pleasantries so far," said Welly. "I'm talking up the dangers of surveying a new route."

Welly was the center of attention. Alys was drawing looks too, enough to make her nudge Marcus into putting an arm around her. Landry stepped forward to crowd away a miner getting too close to Welly's side.

Listening to the conversation helped him realize that this was English. The rhythm and structure were more what he was used to than anything he'd heard in the Spanish or Xhosa speaking parts of Fiera. Certain words became clear. When a miner served tea he was able to say "baigz" understandably enough to receive a smile in return.

When a miner raised his hand toward Welly, Zahm slapped him on the forearm and ordered him and the other younger one out. Then he spoke in a more serious tone.

Welly translated, "He apologizes for their rudeness. It's lonely working here. We should get down to business. Zahm wants to know if you accept the apology."

"I think it matters more if you accept it."

"Oh, I've had worse at any spaceport bar," Welly said cheerfully.

Alys muttered, "That's why I don't go to those bars."

"We accept it," said Landry.

Picking samples of the cargo had been left to Marcus and Alys. They started with food. Zahm's assistant Nail fetched spoons.

A mixed berry jam was offered first. Nail found some pressed crackers to spread it on. The miners bit into them simultaneously.

Both wore ecstatic looks as the sweetness hit their tongues.

Guess they don't have much luxury food stored, thought Landry.

Zahm picked up his spoon, ready to dig into the jam jar, then put it down. "He can't afford to trade for nonessentials," translated Welly.

"Tell him if we make a practical deal I'll throw in a few jars as a present."

Other food samples were refused. Zahm didn't want to be tempted. Batteries were of no interest. Hand tools could be made in the refinery. A sewing kit produced a demand to name a price.

Landry looked over the miners' worn jumpsuits. Yes, they needed to patch some spots. "Pull out that bolt of cloth," he told Marcus.

Zahm made a cash offer. But the cash was Corwynt credit tokens. Landry had no clue how to value them. Interrogating the miners enough to judge the economy of their homeworld would take weeks. And they'd have every incentive to exaggerate the purchasing power of the currency.

"We want to barter," he told Welly. "What goods will they offer?"

Ordinary English words Welly could understand even if she couldn't grasp one or two sounds. That didn't work well for obscure elements. Nail solved the confusion by putting a periodic table on the screen. He moved the rows apart. Dots appeared under each square in the lower half.

"Each dot is an ingot ready to be loaded," said Welly.

No wonder these guys can't afford jam. They don't know enough to keep from showing all their cards at the start. Landry didn't let it show. He wouldn't hurt the miners but making the best deal he could for his ship and crew was his job.

"Is this planet rich in Ytterbium?" He tapped the Yb square on the table for clarity.

After a quick exchange Welly said, "No. If a ship reaches its mass limit with more valuable metals the junk ingots stack up."

He hoped Marcus was keeping as good a poker face as he was. The boy had been ten when *Azure Tarn* had carried one of her most valuable cargoes ever: a load of wrecked ship thrusters and robots headed for a smelter which would extract the ytterbium from them.

Fortunately, Welly was too much of a tech to care how much her toys cost, and Alys was new at this. Landry carefully didn't look over his shoulder to check.

Nail turned and shouted at the door. Several miners vanished.

"If your transport fills up why don't you have it come more often?" Landry asked.

Welly returned the translation. "We're not profitable enough to be a regular stop. Ships come when they have a gap in other work."

"Our cargo hold isn't full. Could we deliver some of your inventory for you?"

After the offer was translated Zahm took a slow sip of his tea. Then another.

Nail said something to him. The boss barked back. Then the two stepped into the hallway for a hushed argument.

"Can you make out what they're saying?" Landry asked Welly.

"Not well. Nail wanted to send a request for parts for some broken chewers. Zahm thinks we might fly home with his stuff. Now they're arguing over theft risk versus lost productivity from two chewers down."

Marcus stepped closer. "Would hauling bulk cargo pay enough to be worth the time?"

Landry turned to put his back to their hosts. "The money would be gravy. Hauling ingots is a way to get directions to their planet, have a good excuse for landing there, and meet whoever receives the cargo."

The younger man's poker face relaxed into a smile, then stiffened again. "Yessir. But will they know the way? They're not pilots."

"I'll settle for the emergence point."

They all turned as Zahm and Nail returned. Welly translated the boss' speech.

"We have contractual obligations to ship some products only on ships approved by our broker. But you may carry some of the others."

Not risking the most valuable cargo with a stranger was perfectly sensible. Landry wanted to applaud Zahm for finally making a good negotiating move.

"That's fine. So the deal is some cloth, sewing kits, and food plus hauling metal in exchange for some metal."

Then it was the tedious business of dickering over exact amounts. The main compensation for cargo hauling would be a percentage paid by the broker.

Marcus handled selling the goods. He might not get the best deal, but Landry wanted him to have the practice. He'd be responsible for his own ship someday.

Sitting back and listening let the captain get a better grasp of the miners' accents. As the same words were repeated he could memorize them, and recognize the pronunciation shifts in others.

As they moved into the payment phase Landry pushed for more ingots and said he didn't care which element as much. The miners suggested ytterbium. Zahm offered six ingots of it.

"Ehzp zeegy?" said Landry, hoping he'd gotten 'just six' right.

Zahm sighed and said an unfamiliar word.

"He's offering twelve," said Welly.

"That's fair."

One knot of worry in Landry's belly went away. They were guaranteed a profit for this trip now.

Then it was all shifting cargo. The crane and forklift work were delegated. Landry suited up every couple of hours to stand on the cargo hold aft stairs and watch without commenting. He and the first mate both checked the load balance calculations Marcus entered in the ship's computer.

On his fourth visit to the stairs Landry decided to make comments. The cargo hold was open, the main hatch lowered to make a ramp for the miners' forklifts. Marcus used a flashlight to direct them to the stacks of ingots. Alys used the crane to shift the original cargo to the corners of the hold.

The new addition was Tets. The apprentice mechanic was applying an electric welding torch to a pair of ingots.

The captain went down the ladder and waited for the forklift to leave. He walked over to Marcus and touched helmets. "What's with the welding?"

"Oh, the miners said that's normal. Our tie-downs aren't strong enough to keep the ingots from sliding if we have a strong side-vector. Spot welding them makes a solid block and that we can secure. "

"Right." He didn't have to ask what Tets thought of the extra work. The arc light showed the mechanic's grin clearly in his faceplate.

***

Zahm provided a chart of where their supply ships had emerged from hyperspace. The curve indicated another spiral rift matching the one they came in on. The rest of the course instructions were verbal descriptions of landmarks but Soon was confident she could find their destination.

"As long as we're at the right star the planet is easy."

The rift didn't give them any trouble. They emerged on the far side of Fwynwr Ystaen from the Fieran Bubble.

The bridge crew was silent with appreciation for long moments before they started looking for the target star. A vast expanse of hyperspace was clear. Trailing horsetails emerged from thunderheads and more gently glowing puffs of pastel clouds. Nowhere in the Bubble had such a view.

"There it is," said Soon. "When he said 'bird' I expected something vague you had to squint to make out. This . . ."

The landmark for Corwynt's sun was a phoenix shape, two horsetails forming wings as they emerged from a dark red cloud much the shape of a bird's head and body.

"Let's get going," said the captain. "Cruising speed."

The worries they'd had during the previous leg were mostly gone. Betty still fretted about long incubation period war plagues, but the rest ignored her. Trying to do that kind of quarantine wasn't practical so they'd decided to accept the risk.

Landry's top priority was language training. Or rather, accent training. Welly reluctantly accepted being the teacher.

Alys had recorded the entire visit to the mining station. This gave Welly good examples to work with. Translating new parts of the conversation was a good test of how much progress her students had made.

Landry still had trouble with the 'grace note' sounds.

A card saying 'JUST' went around the table.

"Ehyp," said Landry.

"No, sir," corrected Welly. "You're saying 'ehyp'. It should be 'ehyp.'

"I really can't tell the difference."

"I'll emphasize." She repeated the word several times.

"Vehyp."

"Okay, that's getting the idea. But you're hammering it. Be gentle."

After a few more repetitions, Welly suggested, "Don't move your lips so much as you say it. You're touching your lower lip to your upper incisors. Leave some space between them."

Trying to control his lips as he talked left the captain unable to speak for some minutes.

Practice did help.

After three days they'd all made enough progress for Welly to declare meal time conversations would be in the local accent.

Bowls of stew went around the table. Passing salt and Worcestershire was simple enough in the accent. A few pleasantries were traded. Then the table went quiet. Nobody was confident enough in their skill to bring up a topic.

Welly focused on her stew.

The vacuum gave Betty a chance to bring up her pet issue again. "What are we going to do if someone gets sick? The Evacuation Fleet had reports of extermination plagues. We could wipe out most of the Bubble if we bring something back."

Crew traded looks around the table.

The first mate spoke gently. "Betty. Our ancestors heard rumors of all sorts of terrible things. Historians proved they didn't have any actual evidence for them.

"Because anyone who witnessed it died!"

"There's a whole planet of living people," said Soon. "They weren't exterminated."

"They could be vaccinated or descended from a few immune people." Betty's knuckles were white as she clutched the edge of the table.

"Then they'll be able to treat us if we get sick," said Lane.

"Only if the incubation period is short enough."

The captain ran out of patience. "While we're there you can research it. When we get back to Fiera we'll stay in orbit until the Health Ministry clears us.

Betty took a breath.

She wasn't given a chance to say any more. "And that's what we'd do if we turned back right now. So going on lets us get more data and treatment. Turning back doesn't help any."

The sensor tech looked down at her bowl. She thrust the spoon in and scooped some stew up, splattering gravy on the table.

***

Further meals polished their skills without explosions.

Behind the phoenix they found a rift in the shoals around the star. That led to days of wandering. The star was surrounded by shoals in multiple spheres around it. They had to search for gaps in each sphere to find their way farther in.

"The good news is going back will be faster," said Soon. She rotated the maps of the shoals over her navigation display.

Roger yawned. "Good." He showed the strain of long shifts. The captain had started rotating others into the helm position. Roger insisted on a larger share. His skill did let them explore faster. He could maneuver close to shoals when others would steer wide, reducing the distance to cover.

The search spiral found an irregular gap in the shoal. Wisps blocked the view through it but the radar revealed a gap and then the round surface of another spherical shoal.

The ship crept through the gaps. Roger kept to the center, wary of spikes that might have been missed by the long-range radar. They came out in the familiar void between two spheres.

"Start clockwise," said Soon. "I'll plot the whole spiral when we have the layer measured."

Roger nodded and began moving away from the gap in the outer sphere. There were no wisps here. They could see both spheres clearly.

Ripples of pink and yellow striped them.

Welly sat up at the comm console. "Cut the radar!"

Displays went blank as Betty flipped switches.

"I'm picking up a signal. Lots of interference. Digital. Text only. Repeating." Welly cycled through filters to try to extract more information out of the ragged transmission.

"Got it. 'Corwynt navigation buoy twenty-seven.' That's all it says."

"That's all it needs to," said Captain Landry. Good work, Welly. Can you give me a vector?"

"It's off the port bow. Can't get better with the surface receivers. But if we point the big dish at it we'll have it for sure."

Roger perked up at having a target to aim for. He pivoted *Azure Tarn* until her main dish was pointed toward the source of the signal. Welly guided him in with old fashioned 'hotter-colder' commands rather than try to calculate angles.

The better receiver gave Welly a more detailed look at the signal. "This is bouncing off the outer shell multiple times to get around the horizon. The interference is other copies taking less optimal bounce paths."

"We have a ways to go then," said the captain. "Roger, follow that trail."

"Aye-aye"

Azure Tarn traced a geodesic over the shoals.

***

The buoy floated by a gap torn in the inner sphere. The design was ancient, one still used in the Fieran Bubble. Just a powerful omnidirectional radio and a long duration power pack.

Passing through the gap exposed the signal of Buoy 23. It marked another gap. On the other side of that was Buoy 19, which announced itself as the marker for transition to normal space.

Spines slumped with fatigue became alert.

Landry felt their eagerness. But . . . the crew had been on duty for eighteen hours picking their way through shoals.

"All hands," he said on the PA. "We've found the marker for entry to the Corwynt system. Meeting them will make for a busy day, so we're going to heave to and run minimum manning for a sleep shift."

A couple of the bridge crew made small disappointed noises but most had enough sense to be relieved.

"We'll return to full manning at 0900. I'll take first watch. See you in the morning."

***

Pastel ripples turned black. Then stars appeared.

Landry gripped his seat until his jump-induced vertigo passed. Then he scanned the bridge crew to make sure they were all right. They were. Soon hadn't even unfolded her sick bag.

"I have two navigation beacons," reported Welly.

Soon checked their vectors. "They're marking the safe zone between shoals."

"Nice to know they're not cheapskates," said the captain. He bit back a demand for more information. Welly would share as she figured it out.

"There's a lot of traffic here,' said the comm tech. She wrestled with her controls.

After a minute Welly continued, "I'm pretty sure I have the planet identified. Let's put the dish on it."

A few minutes work lined them up. More data streamed in.

"Ah. This signal's for us." She put it on the speaker.

"—and intentions. Repeating. Unknown vessel, this is Corwynt System Traffic Control. Your transponder is out. State your identity and intentions. Repeating—"

The voice was rich and cultured. It had a smoother version of the accent they'd learned from the miners.

"Put me on," said Captain Landry.

Welly turned a few switches then gave him a thumbs-up.

"Corwynt System Traffic Control, this is *Azure Tarn* carrying refined metals from Fwynwr Ystaen Mining Station. My apologies for transponder failure. Request vector to Bundoran City Landing Field. *Azure Tarn* out."

Betty said, "The transponder is in perfect working order."

"Yes, but it's not responding to the local ping codes. Figure out if you can modify it or if we want to buy a local one."

"Yes, sir."

"Acknowledged, *Azure Tarn*. Welcome to Corwynt. Vector will be sent on subchannel five."

"Thank you, Control." Landry drew a finger across his throat.

Welly cut the transmission.

"See? No problem. We came in from a known port with a normal cargo and nobody cares that we have a funny accent."

Lane shot him a 'stop gloating' glare.

"Vector received. Transferring to Nav," reported Welly.

Soon typed for a couple of minutes before passing judgement on Traffic Control's directions. "It works. Restricts our acceleration profile. We'll take over a day to get there. Takes us around the planet twice before landing."

"Keep us on the rails," said the captain.

"Aye-aye," answered Roger.

***

Attention shifted from scanning radio traffic to looking at the planet as they drew closer.

"Is there any land?" demanded Betty.

"There's lots of islands. See the city lights on the night side?" Soon pointed to an irregular chain of dots.

"I'm amazed the cities survive." Roger's voice was awed. He'd focused on the hurricanes dominating the illuminated side of the planet. "How strong are those storms?"

Captain Landry had done weather spotting when visiting the Bubble's less developed planets. "All three are category five. Or maybe they've created higher categories here."

The tropical and temperate zones of the planet were dominated by the spiral formations of huge hurricanes. The dark blue of deep ocean shone between them. One straddled the terminator, half hidden by night.

Corwynt's moon was bare rock. It reflected enough sunlight on the night side of the world to reveal two more hurricanes, as massive as the others.

The night side city lights were all concentrated, lacking the dimmer suburbs of Fiera's cities.

As they crossed to day side again Soon pointed out their destination. "That's Bundoran. It's an hour past dawn there."

"We're landing on a dot?" grumped Betty.

The captain chuckled. "It's not that big a ship."

Completing their first circuit of the world revealed a sixth hurricane.

"Why the hell would anyone live here?" said Betty.

"Water worlds are scarce," said Landry. "Colonists can't be fussy."

He resolved to restrict Betty to the ship until they'd developed a feel for what the locals would be offended by. He didn't need the sensor tech starting a war with her bad attitude.

The next loop around the planet made them appreciate their luck in Bundoran being clear of the hurricanes. *Azure Tarn's* engines could power through a storm but landing in such weather could bend the gear.

Traffic Control's prescribed path didn't take them through a storm. They flew through the upper atmosphere over one, too high to feel its winds. Then the vector angled down straight to Bundoran.

"I see the island," reported Roger. "Can't see the city."

"Coordinates are on the north side," said Soon.

Captain Landry focused on keeping his mouth shut. His crew was doing fine. Micromanaging would just make things worse.

Welly handled coordination with the spaceport. "They want to know when you have a visual on the field."

"I haven't even spotted the city yet," complained Roger.

Lane sat up at her console. "Yes, you have. That's not a mountain. It's an arcology. A city in one big building."

"That's . . . it can't be." Roger looked between the radar display and the view out the bridge window.

"Look at the shape. It's a pyramid with a rounded top. Designed to stand up to hurricanes. The sides are too flat to be natural."

Welly drew in a breath. "How many people can fit in there?"

"I don't know how densely they live. Millions, maybe."

Roger expanded the flat part of the island on the radar display. "That makes these things ships and hangars then."

Captain Landry turned to Welly. "Tell them we have visual."

As they drew closer the pyramid's nature became apparent. Rows of windows revealed indoor trees. Aircraft flew out of hatches halfway up the sloped wall. Antenna of varied shapes were scattered over the dome topping the structure.

Roger said, "I'm surprised there's no balconies."

"The hurricanes would rip them off," responded Lane.

The spaceport was the normal flat expanse of concrete. Painted circles indicated landing spots. Straight stripes restricted paths for ground vehicles. The perimeter was lined with hangars. These weren't the thin metal walled structures used back home. Corwynt hangers were slope-sided and built of concrete.

An old-fashioned windsock showed the angle of the stiff breeze blowing over the spaceport. It didn't bother Roger at all. He brought *Azure Tarn* down gently as a first kiss

Landry wasn't sure they were down until Roger shut down the thrusters, their hum deepening into silence.

"Permission to shift to local?" asked Lane.

"Granted," said the captain.

The artificial gravity stopped. Landry waved his arm to judge the difference. At only seven percent less than Fieran standard it was barely noticeable.

Welly notified the spaceport control tower of their arrival. "Could you relay a message from us to the local net?"

She checked the note on her screen while waiting for the answer. "Thank you. Please notify Vychan Goch that we have a cargo from Fwynwr Ystaen for him." A pause. "Thank you."

Welly took her headset off and turned to face the captain. "An Inspector is on the way. Other than that we're set."

"Good. Welly, you have first watch. Let's go take a look at the place."

Lane notified the rest of the crew, reminding them to keep quiet. The captain still reached the forward airlock first. He swung it open and stepped into the morning sunlight.

The ocean here had the same salt smell as Fiera's. The whiff of burnt hydrocarbons Landry was used to in industrial areas was missing. Instead there was an oily, fishy scent he couldn't place.

He'd expected to smell some rot from a marsh. Instead the air was as clean as a sailboat in mid-ocean.

Landry wiped sweat from his forehead. The air was tropical despite Bundoran's middle latitude. The air was too humid for any sweat to dry. He'd have to get his summer clothes out of the storage locker. Some of the crew might have to make cut-offs of their jumpsuits.

Marcus stepped up next to his father. "No wheels," he muttered.

Landry followed his gaze. All the ground vehicles scooting around the spaceport floated on antigrav. On Fiera antigrav was reserved for emergency vehicles and VIP transports. Here even the cargo hauler with two shipping containers on its flat platform hovered on shimmering air.

One floater turned off the traffic lane to their pad. It was a two seater. The forward seat held a driver in a rough vest over bare skin and a floppy tan hat, his own protection a low windscreen. The rear seat was an enclosed cylinder only big enough for one.

The driver aimed straight for the crew. Just as Landry readied to pull Lane and Marcus clear the floater pivoted, slid to a stop, and settled to the pavement with the door of the rear compartment facing them.

It popped open. A young man with dark Asiatic features stepped out. He wore a deep blue tricorn hat with gold trim, held on against the breeze with a braided gold chinstrap. The heavy jacket had more gold braid on the cuffs and epaulets. A multicolored ribbon sat over one breast pocket, an asymmetric silver pin over the other. A yellow stripe went down each side of the black pants. The boots were tall and shiny and, of course, black.

"I am Ensign Koing, the Censorial Inspector. You should know that while there are worlds in the Censorate where laxness is permitted in law enforcement, this is not one of them. Who is the master of this vessel?"

He stepped forward and bowed. "Sir, I'm Niko Landry, master of the *Azure Tarn*. Thank you for your welcome."

Landry didn't feel any respect for the inspector—the kid was younger than Marcus—but this kind needed to be buttered up so they wouldn't feel the need to exert their authority. What kind of government was a 'Censorate'? And were all their officials like this?

"Is this your whole crew?"

"All but the technician on bridge watch."

The ensign frowned.

Landry turned to Marcus. "Ask Welly to join us."

The boy dashed for the airlock intercom.

"We're mostly carrying refined metals from Fwynwr Ystaen, but there's some other cargo. I have a complete inventory." Landry tugged a flimsy from his thigh pocket and unfolded it.

"Any contraband?"

"No, sir," Landry said firmly. Maybe too firmly. Was the kid fishing for a bribe? No, the corrupt ones always started off friendly.

The ensign ignored the flimsy. His gaze drifted over the crew.

Landry put the flimsy back in his pocket. He wondered if the inspector would insist on a visual examination of the cargo.

Running boots sounded through the airlock. Welly emerged. Landry could hear her panting.

The ensign's mouth twitched up in a hint of a smile.

You like making people hop when you say frog, do you? thought Landry.

"You will all register with the planetary index." The officer produced a palm-sized flat gadget. "Place your thumbprint in the center. Hold it while stating your name and the name of your ship."

As was proper the captain went first. "Niko Landry. *Azure Tarn*."

He stepped aside to make room for the first mate. Rubbing the ball of his thumb smeared a barely visible drop of blood. Had the gadget injected something? Or taken a sample? Either way it didn't hurt.

The crew rotated through efficiently. When sweat drops landed on the gadget the ensign wiped it clean with a handkerchief.

Landry wished he'd brought a cloth to wipe his face. Swiping his hand over his forehead sent stray drops into his eyes. The salt stung. He was glad he'd worn a short sleeve shipsuit. A formal outfit would give him heat stroke.

Not that the Censorial officer seemed bothered by the heat.

When the last crewman intoned, "Welly Smat. *Azure Tarn,*" the officer tucked the gadget away again.

"Thank you for your cooperation," said the officer. "If you need any assistance contact Spaceport Control."

He pivoted on his heel and marched back to the two seater. A black box clung to the center of the jacket. Hairs on the back of his neck waved in the breeze blowing out of the collar.

Crap, thought Landry. *These guys would rather wear portable coolers than dress for the weather.*

The inspector and his driver left with a barely audible hum.

"That was strange," declared Lane.

Landry nodded. "Didn't ask about our itinerary, didn't look at the cargo. Least curious customs guy I ever saw."

"Was he customs?" asked Marcus. "He just cared about people. Felt like Immigration or law enforcement."

Gander grumbled, "It's too hot to care. The thruster's due for a tear down. Let's get started." A jerk of his thumb sent Tets into the ship ahead of him. The apprentice looked back over his shoulder at the fascinating new world as he went through the airlock.

Over the next hour most of the crew went back into the cool of the spaceship. The Bundoran spaceport didn't look that different from the ones back home except in its stolid hurricane-proofing.

Landry kept watching. He could do that without creating a traceable record in the planetary data network. He soaked up the size of the ships in port, the efficiency of loading and unloading, and the traffic to the monolithic city.

The people mostly fell into two categories—ornately uniformed government people supervising or interrupting work, and locals wearing hats and sometimes not much else. The locals were a consistent ethnic group, sharp straight-nosed faces with a coffee-with-two-creams complexion. The government ones had every kind of face Landry had seen before and a few not found in the Fieran Bubble. The handful of spacers from other worlds were as varied as the uniformed ones.

Walking around his ship let Landry survey the rest of the spaceport. Traffic wasn't overwhelming it. Only half the hangars had a ship in them. The landing circles on the flat expanse were three quarters empty. Past the hangars he could see a fleet of sailing ships with yellow sails headed toward the city.

A floater turned off the lane into *Azure Tarn*'s landing circle. It slowed, not making the aggressive approach of the inspector's craft. The driver sat on a bench wide enough for three. The rear was a square open-topped cargo compartment, not holding anything big enough to stick up over the sides.

It stopped a dozen yards away. "Is this *Azure Tarn*?" called the driver.

"Aye," answered Landry.

The driver hopped out and walked forward, hand extended. He wore a short sleeve shirt and pants stopping just above his knee. They were made of shimmering fabric in complementary shades of grey. A green vest was decorated with white piping. Pockets held markers and a hand screen. His head was protected by a conical hat held on with a string under the chin.

"Greetings! I'm Vychan Goch. Heard you had something for me."

He took Landry's hand in both of his. The captain brought his left up for a full double-handed clasp. The broker was an inch or two below Landry's six feet. Grey hair and smile lines around the mouth and eyes said age, but he still had a firm grasp.

"We came from the far side of Fwynwr Ystaen. We're being paid in metal to transport some of their output here. We have some cargo of our own that might be of interest." Landry waved toward the cargo hatch, now open to let the sea breeze blow some of the musty air out of their life support system.

Vychan stepped forward. "I didn't know there was anything past there. The Censorate says it is a dead end."

"We, ah, stumbled over a new route."

"By-passing the Censorial tariffs. That could be profitable, until they cover the gap." The local said this with a slight smile.

"If we can find the right partnerships to make it work."

"I'm sure we can." Vychan cocked his head at the other crew standing outside.

Landry introduced them. "Mr. Goch, this is the ship's first mate, and my wife, Lane. Our son Marcus. And Spacer Vissen."

Vychan Goch shook hands all around. "Delighted to meet you. Welcome to Corwynt. I'm glad to see you have a family crew."

"Just the three of us are family. The rest are contract crew." Though Alys seemed to want to change that.

"Ah. Would you be willing to say they are family? That would make things easier when they're off-ship."

Landry glanced at his wife. She nodded. "Certainly," he said. "Unless there's penalties for misrepresenting a relationship?"

'No, no, it's an expected fiction. But it allows the law to turn miscreants over to you for punishment."

"Then they're my cousins."

"Good. Now let's see this cargo."

Marcus handled the tour of the cargo hold. Vychan took notes on his screen. Alys helped with the speculative cargo, using the overhead crane to lift the top items off stacks to reveal the pallets underneath.

The ship had a full inventory of the cargo. Trying to transfer that from *Azure Tarn's* core to Vychan's gadget failed. Vychan set up a data connection with the spaceport. Only basic text worked but that let a message go through.

"We may extract extra value for the foods for their novelty. An auction would maximize that, but I'll need time to set it up. How long do you plan to be on world?"

"We don't have a schedule. We can stay a few weeks to maximize the profit." *And find out as much about this Censorate as we can.*

"On an open pad? If you stay through the next storm you'll need a hangar."

Landry chuckled. "I'd take a hangar. But we don't have any cash to rent one."

"You will. That Ytterbium isn't enough to cover the standard shipping fees for this much mass. I'll deposit the difference into an account for you." Vychan tapped on his screen. "A temporary account? Or do you want to reserve some cash for your next visit?"

"We'll be back. But I'd rather convert everything to goods when we leave."

"Of course." The broker was unsurprised. "There. Deposit will go through as soon as we unload the ingots. When can we do that?"

"Now."

"I'll call my nephew."

The nephew and a few other members of the Goch family arrived with three floaters, two cargo haulers, and a mid-size vehicle holding a forklift on treads. Landry was relieved to see Corwynt's cheap antigravity couldn't handle every function.

The Gochs were efficient. The stacks of ingots were offloaded in half the time it had taken to bring them on. As the forklift was loaded onto its carrier again, Vychan turned to Landry.

"My clan can't feed your whole crew on this short notice but we can squeeze in two or three. May I treat you to dinner, Captain?"

"Certainly. Let me see who else is available." Landry jerked his head at his first mate. They moved to the side to discuss it. Vychan obligingly had Marcus lead him back to the stack of speculative cargo.

"If you're asking me out to dinner, I say yes," said Lane.

Landry gave her a wry smile. "I'd love to. But not yet. I want you here in command in case Vychan pulls a fast one. We don't know a thing about him or this planet."

"Welly found a text-only news feed we can get through that connection. There's even a weather forecast."

"Good." He looked over the forecast, which was unsurprisingly focused on hurricane movements. "Find out everything you can. I'm going to bring Marcus for his education. And in case it gets ugly—Tets."

Lane pursed her lips. "Gander is a better brawler than Tets."

"Yeah. But he starts too many fights. Tets does as he's told."

"All right. Shall I get some pistols out of the armory?"

The captain shook his head. "Not until we know the rules here. We'll have knives. It's easier to claim ignorance with them."

***

Landry shared the floater's bench with Vychan. Marcus and Tets sat in the back, their elbows resting on a toolbox. The massive side of the city rose above them. The wall was smooth. Lines of windows and hatches showed but didn't rise above the surface.

They were headed for a tunnel, the smallest of the openings where the structure met the spaceport. The hatch to close it during storms rested against the wall. Landry studied it as they went through. It was three feet thick at the edge. The center held crisscrossing girders to strengthen it against tidal surges.

The forecast guaranteed no hurricanes would hit Bundoran in the next six days. Landry resolved to move his ship into a hangar sooner rather than later.

A glowing strip down the center of the tunnel roof shed bright light. It still felt gloomy after the cloudless sky over the spaceport.

It was hard to tell how fast they were going. At least twice the speed they'd used in the spaceport. A truck flew past in the other direction too fast for him to get a look at it.

Then they were out of the tunnel in a park. Sunlight shone through the clear wall high above. People picnicked under the trees. A game or brawl rolled across the grass.

It took Landry a moment to realize the sky overhead was painted on the ceiling. The interior of the pyramid was half open space, half smaller pyramids stacked with their corners on the peaks of the ones below.

Vychan turned right at an intersection in the park. They were pointed at a truncated pyramid painted in pastel greens and blues with brown rectangles. Balconies and glowing windows interrupted the curves of color.

The entry had a less robust version of the hatch closing off the outside of the city. The inside had only artificial light and was broken up into substructures each about the size of Landry's ship. Animated signs bore a mix of news and advertisements.

"Welcome to East Docks!" declared Vychan. "Goch Home is right over there."

He pointed at an upper level block. The vehicle elevator was a large ring carrying the floater up a triangular shaft. Then they were getting out at a door.

Or rather a hatch. The wall was sloped in. The door was more solid than the pressure hatches on *Azure Tarn*. Well, those only had to hold one atmosphere of force. Landry was impressed that they needed to build to be stormproof even inside the city.

Goch Home was a flurry of introductions, too many names for Landry to catch. He did memorize Vychan's wife's name, Emlyn.

When the commotion died down (you'd think the man had been away from home for a month. Or did everyone want to see the off-worlders?), Vychan sniffed the air. "What's cooking for dinner?"

"Dinner will be late," said Emlyn. "The Jaaphisii have brought a kraken into port. We're waiting for the market to open."

Vychan turned to the Fierans. "You are lucky men. We'll introduce you to the best of our food."

A young woman said, "Papa, we should go down now and be ready when they open."

"Very well," said Vychan. His wife nodded and tossed her daughter a small sack.

"Do you two feel up to carrying the cut?" the youngster asked Marcus and Tets. Wynny, that was her name.

The boys eagerly agreed. Well, she was cute. Marcus looked to his father for permission. Landry nodded.

***

Wynny filled the trip to the fish market with questions about living in space. Marcus answered without revealing they'd come from outside the Censorate, per his father's orders. Tets stayed silent.

An elevator took them down to the base of the pyramid. Wynny led them down a corridor that had a salt air tang.

Nothing in this city was bare concrete or metal, Marcus noticed. This corridor was decorated with monstrous sea creatures. She pointed to a many-tentacled thing dwarfing the sailboats harpooning it. "That's a kraken. We're picking up a filet of it for the family's dinner."

"A native species?" asked Marcus.

"Uh-huh. The ecology is mostly compatible with humans. Don't eat something you pull out of the sea at random. But the Jaaphisii know what's good to eat."

"Who are the—Jaaphisii?" asked Marcus, fumbling over the unfamiliar word.

"The sailors. They live at sea." The corridor widened out into a harbor. Sailing ships were tied up at the piers.

Marcus stared at the ships. He'd seen sailboats on Fiera. They had wood hulls and woven sails. These ships were strange to him. The sails had veins on them. The hulls looked organic.

The center pier didn't have a ship. The kraken floated there, twice the length of the largest ship in harbor. Hawsers wrapped around the tentacles to hold it in place. A severed tentacle lay on the pier. Men with knives as long as they were tall sliced it into chunks.

"They've opened the market!" exclaimed Wynny. She led them to the crowd at the base of the pier.

Marcus felt useful at last. He wasn't as tall as Tets but he still had enough mass to shield Wynny from the jostling of the crowd. She took advantage of her protectors to force her way through the mob.

The merchants at the tables looked like a different ethnic group. Marcus looked closer. No, they had similar faces to Bundoran's residents but their skin was darkened and roughened from a life on the sea.

"Twenty green for hundred weight," said the old woman at

Wynny's table, spitting the words out like bullets.

"I don't want tentacle meat," replied Wynny. "The filet below the eye. One thirty weight."

"Oooh, someone wants the savory. It'll cost you."

As the merchant gestured Marcus realized she wasn't old, no older than his mother. Her face was so lined and weathered he'd misjudged her age.

Wynny took red and gold striped plastic disks from the sack she carried and laid them on the table.

"No so rude as some city folk you are. Five more."

"Do I look like a Censorial?" She put down two more.

The older woman glared. "I said five."

"Will you let it rot waiting for rich folk to come down from the upper levels? You're not the only fleet to call here."

"Feh." The coins went into a sack under the table. A stream of orders sent four knife wielders trotting toward the swollen end of the tentacle on the pier.

The trio slid over to an empty spot while the merchant began her next dicker. Wynny tapped the plastic disk hanging from her shoulder on a strap. "You'll have to carry the meat through the crowd, but once we have some room I can put it on the minifloat."

Marcus nodded. He watched more flensers peeling the skin off the kraken's head. As one piece caught the sunlight he recognized the vein pattern. "They make their sails from that!"

"Yes. The ships are all made from the sea monsters." Wynny pointed to ships. "That one's hull is a leviathan shell. The masts are spines from megasharks. And there's a triton skeleton with scales to waterproof it."

"Wow. Do they build their houses from them too?"

"They don't have houses. Just ships."

"So they don't live on land at all?"

"Just when they come into port to sell a catch. They'll buy some parts and tools, drink up the rest of the money, and be on their way."

That jolted Tets out of his silence. "They don't keep any money?"

"If they have money, they get taxed. This way the Censorials can't touch them. That's how they want it." Her voice was wistful.

"Jealous?" asked Marcus.

"Not really. Do you see any Jaaphisii here older than that merchant?"

Marcus had been watching. "No."

"There usually aren't. It's a hard life. But they're free."

Two young Jaaphisii staggered up with a slab of yellowish meat weighing more than Tets. It was sloppily wrapped in clear plastic. They slapped it onto the table.

"Gentlemen," said Wynny.

Even with the crane doing most of the work, cargo hauling had put muscle on Marcus. He was glad of it now. Tets was four inches taller and in better shape and his face still showed the strain of heaving the load.

The crowd was nice enough to make way for them. Marcus' arms were screaming when they reached an open spot. Wynny tossed down her disk. It unfolded into an X. The boys centered the slab of meat and lowered it down.

The shoulder strap was now a leash from one end of the X. Wynny squeezed it and the whole assembly lifted a few inches off the floor.

Tets was astonished. Marcus tried to keep his poker face. He looked around and saw a few other customers towing their purchases away on antigrav. No one seemed surprised. That said the devices were cheap enough the Landrys would be able to buy a hundred of them at least. And a hundred antigrav generators would sell on Fiera for enough to buy a new ship.

"Oh, damn. The rush started." The corridor they'd come through was packed with people. Wynny turned right along the docks.

They passed a couple of closed hatches. When they reached an open one Wynny tugged on the leash and the meat followed her in. The boys walked beside her. This one wasn't as decorated. The walls were plain tan. Niches in the walls held live plants every few yards. Some had tendrils drooping almost to the ground.

A cross-corridor branched off to the right. As the trio passed it a clipped voice called, "Cityfolk, let's have thanks."

Wynny mumbled a curse.

A tall young Jaaphisii strode up to them with a rolling gait. He wore loose shorts and a pocketed vest. Harsh sun had burned his arms and legs despite their darkness. He wasn't wearing a hat but the smooth tone of his face said he did at sea. His expression was angry, predatory, hungry. "Thank us Jaaphisii for your dinner."

Marcus stepped in front of Wynny. "Thank you. We appreciate the food you've brought us."

"Nice. Now apologize for the two men who died catching it for you." The sailor loomed over Marcus, hands at his waist.

The spacer didn't give ground. He tilted his head up to look the Jaaphisii in the eye. "I'm sorry you lost your friends. We weren't told about it."

Marcus felt relief as the stranger pivoted away from him. He could hear Wynny talking into her screen.

"How about you, tallboy? Are you sorry?" The Jaaphisii focused on Tets now. The mechanic was an inch or two taller. The sailor displayed muscle earned hauling on ropes and climbing masts.

Tets displayed his palms in a conciliatory pose. "Sure. I'm sorry you lost your guys. I'll pour a drink out for them."

"And will you buy me a drink?"

"Yes. Next time we're in a bar together."

"Liar." The Jaaphisii slammed both fists into Tets' gut. The mechanic had expected more insults first. He landed on his ass.

"Hey!" Marcus charged forward, grabbed the Jaaphisii's arm, and tried to pull him off balance. It was like tugging on a tree branch. A yank from the arm sent his face into the wall of the corridor. Stars filled his vision as he slid down to his knees.

Tets sprang back to his feet and swung at the attacker. Both men landed more blows than they blocked. Drops of red blood landed on the wrapped yellow meat.

Marcus pushed on the wall to get back to his feet. He watched the fight as his head cleared. There was no way he wanted to be in the middle of the blows, he'd be crushed.

As the sailor dodged one of Tets' attacks Marcus saw his chance.

He kicked out, catching the back of the Jaaphisii's knee.

The stumble wasn't large but it let Tets slip the edge of his hand through to slam on the sailor's neck. That made the stumble a stagger. A double-handed blow on the neck sent the Jaaphisii limp to the floor.

Tets bent over, hands on knees, to catch his breath. "Thanks for," pant, "the assist."

"No problem. You okay?"

"I've had worse." Tets poked at a split on his lip.

Marcus flinched as Wynny shoved a handkerchief into his face. "You're bleeding," she cried.

Marcus tried to hold still under the scrubbing. "It's just my nose."

"How can you tell? There's blood all over your face. Didn't your father ever tell you to pick on people your own size?"

"No. He taught me to take care of our crew."

Wynny rolled her eyes. "Men."

Flashing lights announced the arrival of a police floater. Two policewomen in riot gear stood on an open platform, holding the railing on the front edge.

"A Jaaphisii started the brawl early," called Wynny.

A cop laughed. "Haven't even opened up the booze yet. Looks like you handled him. Let's load him up."

Marcus found himself holding the Jaaphisii's feet while Tets hauled on his shoulders. They dumped him roughly onto the floater. One cop wrapped a wire loosely around the brawler's wrists. The other inspected the men's hands and faces.

"Ow," said Tets. "Gently on the knuckles please."

"Just checking who did the work. Excuse me a moment. Don't go anywhere." The two policewomen began a whispered conversation.

Tets leaned down to ask Marcus, "Are we in trouble?"

"Don't think so. Self-defense. Local witness on our side. We might have a lot of paperwork to fill out."

The cop who'd examined them took off her helmet, revealing long braids of red-brown hair wound around her skull. She hung her torso armor on the railing of the floater. The black fatigues underneath clung to a curvy figure.

She waved Marcus away. He retreated to stand next to Wynny.

"I'm Hywel," said the cop. "What's your name?"

"Tets Longshore."

"You handled that pretty well. Have you dealt with obnoxious drunks before?"

"I've been in a few brawls. I never throw the first punch."

Marcus noticed the cop lifting her hands to fiddle with the fatigues. Wynny was turning her head away to hide a smirk.

Hywel asked, "Are you trained in martial arts?"

"No, just learned the hard way." Tets leaned back as the cop pressed into his personal space. "Got tired of being beat up."

"Have you ever thought of being a police officer?"

She grabbed the corners of her collar with both hands and spread them apart. The unbuttoned front of her fatigues flipped open. Marcus couldn't see what was underneath with her back to him. He could see Tets' eyes widen as he stared, snap back up to the cop's face, then drop down again.

Hywel continued, "I'd be happy to bring you into the police force. We could talk about it later when I get off shift."

"Um . . . well, I'd like that . . . maybe . . . I don't know," stammered Tets.

"You're not married, or engaged, are you?"

"Oh, no."

"So . . . who should my uncle talk to?"

Tets didn't have an answer to that. But she did have his full attention.

Wynny broke in. "His family head is dining at Goch Home tonight. That's what this filet is for."

"That's good, thank you."

The other policewoman yelled, "We got a brawl at entry thirty-four delta."

Hywel took a couple steps backwards. "Drop me a line, okay?" She blew Tets a kiss then turned and trotted to the floater, buttoning her fatigues as she went.

She was still donning the riot gear as the floater disappeared around a bend.

"Did she want a job interview or a date?" asked Tets plaintively.

Wynny cocked her head. "What's the difference?"

The boys traded looks. Neither wanted to try answering.

"Anyway, thank you both for dealing with that Jaaphisii. I wouldn't have liked being alone when he came out of that corridor." She picked up the leash of the mini-floater and started walking.

The spacers followed.

***

It hadn't taken much work for Landry to get Vychan complaining about Censorial taxes. "And it's obvious they make it that complicated to just humiliate us. They'd extract more money if they didn't put us through all the hoop-jumping."

The hatch opened, letting in Wynny, a floating slab of meat, and his son and the man who was supposed to protect him, both bloody from a beating.

Landry's chair clattered to the floor as he snapped to his feet. "What did you do?" he demanded of Tets.

Marcus stepped between them. "Captain, it's not his fault. A fisherman attacked us."

Wynny said, "A Jaaphisii wanted the blood tax."

"Ah. My apologies, gentlemen," said Vychan. "I should have sent more with you. Normally the nomads don't start such behavior until after midnight."

"Don't worry, we're fine. It looks worse than it is." The last part of Marcus' protest was muffled as a matron with a first aid kit started cleaning his face.

A boy picked up Landry's chair and held it as the captain sat back down.

Vychan leaned close. "I apologize again. It must be a shock to see your boy hurt. I promise we'll take good care of him."

"Thank you. I'm sorry. I expected things to be more civilized here."

"The city is civilized. The Jaaphisii are barbarous. Most can't even read. They spend their time at sea under total discipline. Then they come here, sell their catch, and drink, fight, and screw until the money's all spent."

Landry glanced at his boys. They were donning clean shirts. "I'm surprised you let barbarians in your city."

"Some cities don't. They eat vatmeat and vegetables. We want better food. The price is taverns with busted furniture and men beaten senseless. Plus a few parts and radios for their ships."

"Who'd be stupid enough to go brawl with those maniacs?"

Vychan's eyes flicked up. A smirk appeared and disappeared as quickly. "Jaaphisii women love winners," he whispered.

"Ah."

"I'll say this for them," he said in a normal tone. "It's the perfect tax avoidance scheme. No cash retained to pay taxes with. No records for a headcount. No permanent residence. Market value of their ships is zero. They're totally free from the Censorials."

Landry chuckled. "Ever think of running off to sea?"

"All the young and foolish think it. But it's a hard and dangerous life for those born to it. Learning it as an adult. Well. The Jaaphisii take volunteers. And tell the sad story on their next port call."

Landry thought on that as he looked around the room. The 'living room' of the Goch home had room for all eighty-some Gochs to sit down for a meal together, plus a couple of dozen guests. At the far end was an open kitchen, now producing the scent of frying meat instead of roasting vegetables. The sides were walled off (the first vertical wall he'd seen since leaving his ship) for private bedrooms and suites. Hallways led off to more rooms elsewhere.

Bells chimed at the hatch. A teenage boy let in a uniformed man. The boy pointed toward Landry.

The captain cursed under his breath as the uniformed stranger marched toward him. *How much trouble are those boys in?*

Vychan made the introductions. "Captain, this is Chief Owerth of the East Side Police. Chief, Niko Landry, master of the merchant ship *Azure Tarn*."

The handshake was firm. People moved away to give Owerth a seat and the illusion of privacy.

"I understand the man Tets is one of your crew?"

"Yes, sir."

"How would you describe him?"

"Cheerful, hard-working, enthusiastic. Not a trouble-maker in any way." *Also lazy and easily distracted but I'm not telling you that.*

"Good. We're very impressed by his performance earlier. The Jaaphisii need to remember that going outside the boundaries just makes it worse for them."

"I'm glad to hear that."

"Is Tets married? Or have an engagement or intention for marriage?"

"No, not married. And I haven't heard of any plans." Landry was certain any marriage with Tets would involve a dozen bottles of whiskey to generate that bad an idea.

"My niece Hywel is taken with him. She's a pretty girl, said he seemed to like her too. If he joins the police I promise he'll be a full officer. Once he has all his training he'll have full legal authority. If he does well and works hard he could have my job someday."

Landry couldn't tell if he was having culture shock or just was misunderstanding the local accent. What did this niece wanting a date have to do with recruiting Tets as a cop, and why would either one be brought to Landry first? He settled for saying, "I don't understand."

"Well, what's confusing about it? We'll pay a good wed-price for him."

Anger flared in Landry. "I'll be damned if I'll sell one—"

Vychan leaned in between the two of them, putting a hand on Landry's. "Gentlemen, if you'll forgive my interruption, I think I can help resolve the confusion."

He waited until Landry and Chief Owerth settled down before continuing. "The captain doesn't know of marriage plans for Tets because it's not him who makes the plans. It's your aunt, if I remember right, yes?"

Landry didn't understand this but trusted Vychan enough to give a nod.

"So you see, Chief, the captain won't know if Tets is available until they return to their homeworld. No offense to your lovely young lady, or fuss over the wed-price. It's just travel."

"That's a shame. If he is still available I can't guarantee Hywel will be unwed when you next visit our world. I'd be delighted to introduce him to other young ladies of the police."

"Thank you," was the safest thing Landry could think of to say.

The police chief stood up and adjusted his equipment belt. "I've my own share of Jaaphisii heads to break tonight. Best get back to it."

"You're not dining with us?" said Vychan.

"Too much work and not enough of us to do it. Which is why I'd like your Tets on the force, Captain. Well met."

When the hatch slammed shut behind the policeman Vychan's wife Emlyn said, "They are getting desperate if they're entrapping off-worlders."

Laughter went up among the tables. Wynny said, "Officer Hywel was young for an old maid they need to bid higher for," to even more laughter.

Vychan took pity on Landry's confusion. "It's been a joke here for years. The police need big strong men to deal with the brawlers, right? Well in Wynny's generation all their children were girls. Nearly two dozen girls in a row. Good at policing in normal times but they don't scare the Jaaphisii into behaving. Owerth is searching for husbands to beef up his force."

That fit with the other piece Landry had heard, but— "To be a cop here you have to be born into it, or marry in?"

A teenage girl ladled some leafy vegetables onto their plates. A boy following behind added stir-fried kraken.

"Aye. Just as your son was born into flying a ship and your wife married into it." Vychan dug in.

Landry followed his example. The meat was intensely savory, with just enough sour overtone to keep it from overwhelming him. Landry chewed slowly to appreciate it. "Yes, but that's unusual on Fiera. Most businesses are unrelated people working together."

Vychan nodded. "You're like the Censorials then. We see their inefficiency. No one is motivated to help each other by relationships so they have to use bribery and favor-trading to get cooperation."

"It works for us," said Landry defensively.

"Oh, I'm not criticizing you, I apologize if I sounded like that. I'm just happy to work with my family."

The captain waved at the crowd. "Everyone here is a broker?"

"More work in the warehouses than the brokerage. And Goch Home takes much work to run. But yes, we're all one business."

He pointed at his daughter, laughing at something Marcus said. "Look at Wynny. She could be an accountant at the brokerage or do inventory in a warehouse. When she marries we'll teach her husband to drive a fork-lift. Or if she marries out we'll have the wed-price to cover the losses while someone else learns the work."

Another delicious bite of kraken gave Landry time to think about this. "How does it work for big companies?"

Vychan shrugged. "There's not many bigger than two hundred. A family of three or four hundred has a lot of bickering. They'll split it into two companies."

"Sir?" Tets stood by Landry. "Am I in trouble?"

Landry let him sweat a moment before answering. "He wanted to give you a life sentence . . . but I talked him out of it."

The mechanic gulped. "Um, thank you, sir."

"Enjoy your meal."

Tets retreated back to the table holding the twenty-somethings.

"We're showing you more of the world than I planned," said Vychan. "I hope you're enjoying it."

"I am. We came here to learn." He took another bite of the salty vegetables, and finally placed when he'd eaten something similar. "Is this seaweed?"

"Aye. The shoalers around here farm it, and they're cheaper than the hydroponics produce. Mostly by evading the Censorial taxes."

"Are they nomads too?"

"No, no, they each have their own reef or shoal or sandbar to farm. They live in underwater houses, too deep for the storms to hurt them.

And legend has it there's a secret house, deeper down where they put everything they don't want tax collectors to see."

Landry shared in Vychan's laugh. "Is it true?"

"All I know is when I've visited a shoaler they live poorer than someone with that income should."

"So where do the Censorials get their taxes from?"

"Us." Vychan waved to take in the entire pyramidal city they were in. Then he tried to catch up on his eating. Another wave of kraken meat had been served, this time baked with spices.

Landry was still trying to wrap his mind around Corwynt society. "If there's men so eager to brawl with Jaaphisii why aren't they joining the police?"

"Jaaphisii women aren't fond of men who win their brawls with shock-sticks. And married men can't collect the rewards."

"Ah. I see." More kraken was savored. "I have to confess marrying for a job seems unromantic to me."

"There's some of that. More often someone falls in love and takes the job to be together. Is it that much to ask of Wynny's future husband that he drive a forklift for her?"

"No," Landry admitted.

"Oh, there's a great vid I should show you. 'Love and Terror'. A boy falls in love with a girl in the traveling circus. They sneak off to marry. Her parents and grandparents don't like him at all. They find out he's afraid of heights so they make him be an acrobat. So he has to overcome his fear to keep her."

Vychan called to his wife, "Emlyn, could we show our guests 'Love and Terror' tonight?"

"Didn't you hear? Director Bledig died last year."

"No! That's a pity. He was the best vid maker in my life." He turned back to Landry. "We're out of luck, sorry."

"Weren't there copies of the vid?"

Vychan looked like he'd suggested robbing a bank. "Not any more. Art dies with the artist."

Had they destroyed their copy? Given that expression he didn't dare push. Landry thought of old books he'd read, some from before

humanity left Earth. And the Shakespeare performance he'd taken
Lane to as their second date. This difference shocked him more than
the family business rule.

The two older men had been served first. They were finished while
most of the family was still eating.

"I have a bottle I keep in my study," said Vychan in a low voice.
"Would you like to try it?"

A nod brought the two of them to a small room, about the size of
Landry's cabin on the *Azure Tarn*. A leather couch on one wall faced a
desk with a comfortable chair and multiple display screens. Shelves and
cabinets covered the walls. Printouts, manufacturer's samples, models,
and pictures filled all available space.

A wave sent Landry to the couch. Vychan extracted an amber
bottle and two broad glasses from a cabinet. "This has never known
seawater," he said as he poured. "There are some farming islands near
the arctic where this was made."

Landry took the glass by the stem and sniffed. Alcohol smacked his
nose. He hadn't drunk anything that strong in years. As the shock
faded he noticed the more subtle aspects of the scent. Fruit brandy,
very high quality.

He sipped, and lifted the glass in a salute.

Vychan smiled and sipped his own drink.

After a couple of minutes he said, "I've been trying to show you
what Corwynt is like. What do you think of it?"

"I like it. Despite the barbarians. Your culture is too different from
what I'm used to for me to want to live here. But I'm happy to visit.
You're good people."

"Thank you. And of course I'm curious about your home."

Landry used his glass to buy time to think about his answer. He'd
evaded most of the questions about Fiera, afraid some subtle error
would reveal their secret. He'd drawn Vychan out about the Censorate,
finding lots of tax complaints but no overt expressions of disloyalty.
Still . . . he was going to have to trust somebody.

"Fiera was in a bubble that just recently reopened. We've been
sealed away from the rest of the human race for over nine hundred

years. Never heard of Corwynt or the Censorate."

Vychan tossed down the rest of his brandy. "I see. That's what you've been dancing around all day. Here I thought it was something boring such as finding a route around the Censorial tariff patrols."

"No, not that."

"I've never met anyone from outside the Censorate before. They say they rule all of humanity. They're going to get all sorts of excited when they find your world."

"The inspector wasn't excited by us."

"Wouldn't be. Those boys are the dregs. Might never notice you're unusual. But when a survey squadron finds your bubble there'll be a war fleet along in due course."

"I can't stop the survey. But I don't want them to find out from our visit. I just want to trade and go home."

Vychan scratched his chin. "I'll pass the word to not ask where you're from. The family can hold a secret. You might stress the need not to talk about it to your crew. Just the name of the world is all right. We don't know all the worlds in the Censorate."

"Good. I don't want to ever deal with the Censorate."

"You'll need to make peace with them sooner or later. It's too big to escape."

"I'm going to keep a low profile."

***

The next day Landry invited Vychan to lunch at the spaceport tavern. It was far enough from East Docks to be free of Jaaphisii. The food wasn't fine enough to attract Censorials. The slabs of vatmeat on salty bread were still better than the stored rations *Azure Tarn* had left.

Landry and Marcus had just been served when the broker arrived.

"Good day, Captain. And to you, Marcus. You're looking better than I expected. After a beating like that my face was always many colors the next day."

The younger man flushed and rubbed at his face. The eyes were still shadowed despite the bruise cream he'd applied last night.

"And how is Tets?"

"About the same," said Landry. "He can talk without it hurting now."

"A sturdy young man."

The waiter inquired for Vychan's order and was told, "The same." The broker followed on with a list of potential customers he'd contacted about *Azure Tarn*'s cargo.

"Thank you, that's very encouraging," said Landry. "I thought of a favor I would like to ask of you."

"Go on."

"I'd like a history book. Something covering Corwynt and the Censorate back to its founding."

The fried seaweed chip Vychan held snapped in half, pieces sailing to the floor. "Who are you to ask such a thing?"

Landry turned his palms out, hoping the gesture wasn't offensive. "Not asking for a gift. I'm willing to trade." He nodded to Marcus.

His son pulled a school reader out of a thigh pocket. "This is a history of the Fieran Bubble. More than that—it goes all the way back to Earth's pre-history."

Vychan frantically waved it away. Marcus slid it back into the pocket.

The local took a deep breath with his eyes closed. When they opened he was calm again. "I must make this trade. But not here. My cousin Nia has her outing three days from now. Bring as many of your crew as you like. Speak carefully, there will be people from other families there."

"Thank you. We will attend."

Then Vychan began talking up a new vid, a disaster flick showing an arcology city hit by a crashing spaceship just as a hurricane arrived.

Landry responded with a Fieran show about a city threatened by a volcanic eruption. Vychan encouraged him to tell more details until they were all done eating.

"Thank you for a pleasant meal. I must contact some more buyers. You need to think on what you want for a return cargo." Vychan followed with more pleasantries before leaving.

Marcus started to ask a question but his father silenced him with a headshake. *Not here.*

***

Gander wasn't Soon's first choice of a shore leave buddy, but no one else wanted to leave the ship after the captain's "don't say we're from outside the Censorate" speech. One of the new rules was not leaving the ship alone. Shopping for navigation charts likely wasn't Gander's first choice for an outing but he was willing to join her to stretch his legs.

They didn't have any trouble finding the spaceport administration building. It was built into the wall of the city but had multiple hatches facing the port. It had more traffic than even the tavern, spacers looking variously anxious when inbound and frustrated or relieved departing.

Soon guessed right that the center hatch would open into the lobby. Bureaucrats, mechanics, businessmen, and spacers swarmed past them as she studied the directory wall.

"Where to, boss?" muttered Gander.

"Publications, I guess. There's no entries for Survey or Astrography."

He grunted, about as much enthusiasm as she could hope for, and followed her to the second-floor office.

A chairless waiting area was separated by a counter from an array of desks. Only one clerk stood at the counter. Three natives were in line. Soon took her place behind them.

She watched Gander wander off to scan the posters covering the walls of the waiting area. They all had bright red headlines featuring the words 'MANDATORY' or 'FORBIDDEN'.

Soon turned back to face the counter. The clerk wore a powder blue uniform jacket. There weren't any decorations on it. Some of the clerks at the desks did have a ribbon or two on their uniforms.

The clerk seemed determined to misunderstand everyone's requests. It took multiple rephrasings and apologies for the other customers to get what they needed. Soon wondered if he wasn't understanding the local accent. None of the clerks were the same ethnic type as the locals.

Gander stepped back from the posters. "Soon, come take a look at this."

The clerk handed the local a form, waved him aside, and gestured impatiently to Soon. She spoke her request slowly and precisely. "I need a hard copy astrographic chart of this system as a backup. How much would that cost, please?"

The clerk's eyes widened. "How dare you. How dare you! I should have you arrested!"

Soon was speechless. She'd prepared for various responses, particularly being told this was the wrong department, but this was so far beyond her imagining she couldn't respond.

A painful grab on her arm snapped her around. Gander's angry face almost touched her nose. "I told you not to talk to anyone!" he snarled.

Soon couldn't muster a reply to that either.

Gander turned to the clerk and spoke in an obsequious tone. "I'm very sorry, sir. I should have been watching her more closely. What kind of trouble have her delusions caused this time?"

"Attempting to obtain restricted information is a serious offense," said the clerk primly.

"Of course, sir. But she didn't understand what she was saying. She just tries to imitate the real crew. Which is why we need to supervise her. I failed in my duty because I was trying to learn your local regulations." Gander waved at the posters. "Please, sir. The captain will have me flogged if she's punished for my neglect."

A puzzled expression crept across the clerk's face. "Why would you have an insane crew member on your ship?"

"Well, sir, a ship's entertainer doesn't need a sound mind, only a sound body." He waved a hand at Soon's torso.

She bit back an indignant reply. Whatever was going on Gander understood it better than her. She held her complaints for later.

"You outworlders and your disgusting perversions," said the clerk.

"I should never have left home. Go on, don't let me ever see either of you again."

"Yes sir, thank you, sir," said Gander.

Soon struggled to keep her feet as Gander hauled her out of the room. In the hallway she started to ask what the hell happened, but he hissed her into silence. That continued through the elevator and lobby.

Her first lungful of outside air felt like breathing soup. It was still a relief to be out of that building. Gander let go of her arm. Soon rubbed at the sore spot.

"Sorry to be rough on you," he said. "I wanted to get out fast."

She nodded. Bits of the encounter flashed through her mind. Most made no sense. But one piece—"Did you call me a whore?"

"I did. Which saved you from being arrested for soliciting classified information, bribing a Censorial official, and probably resisting arrest. They always like adding resisting arrest. So say thank you."

"Thank you, Chief," Soon said meekly.

"I read the poster prohibiting the sharing of notes on space travel or observations of stellar phenomena. Sorry I don't read faster."

"Thanks."

They walked a bit farther from the administration building. "Why would they restrict charts? They're not blockading or patrolling. We could explore the routes ourselves. What's the point?"

Gander shrugged. "Bureaucratic bullshit. Keeping out everyone without the gumption to do their own survey. Hiding something off the main routes. Maybe all of those. Who knows?"

"And trying to find out would get me arrested."

They approached the intersection between the lane toward the tavern and the one back toward *Azure Tarn*.

"I think I owe you a beer," said Soon. "Or ten beers."

They stood at the corner for a long moment, contemplating what could go wrong in an ordinary transaction at the tavern.

Gander wiped sweat from his forehead. "Tell you what. Sweet-talk the captain into buying a keg for the ship."

She nodded. They turned toward the ship, walking slowly to not overheat.

***

Soon's misadventure discouraged further expeditions. Picnicking in the shade of the ship was enough fresh air for most. Vychan set up an account for deliveries, providing food good enough to eliminate one of the traditional motives for going ashore.

The crew watched a new freighter land. It was an unfamiliar design, flat-bottomed with an oval layout. Marcus' attention drifted back to the city. The sun was high enough to shine through the upper levels. He could see trees silhouetted at one corner.

"We really need to find out what it's like in there," he said.

"In what? The jail cells?" said Betty. Several crew laughed. Soon didn't.

Marcus persisted. "There have to be market opportunities. The kind of stuff a local wouldn't notice."

"And traps a local wouldn't notice," said Gander. He'd shrugged off praise of his rescue, attributing their escape to the bureaucrat's desire to not do extra paperwork.

"So we start out cautious. Just walk around and look. Don't talk to anybody."

The first mate was the senior officer outside. She frowned at her son. "Don't go alone."

"I'll go with you," said Alys.

That didn't cheer up the first mate. But when Marcus said, "Permission to go ashore, ma'am?" she nodded.

***

Marcus decided "yes" and "thank you" didn't count as talking to anyone when a freight floater offered them a lift into the city.

"Spacers?" asked the driver. He was more tanned than most of the locals but didn't have the burnt-dark skin of the Jaaphisii.

"Yes. It's our first time here," Marcus answered.

Alys just nodded.

"Truly. Then go see the waterfall. Second top." He halted the floater as it emerged from the access tunnel.

"Thank you, we will." The two spacers hopped off and returned the driver's wave as he sped away.

Alys asked, "What's second top?"

"Don't know. Let's wander until we see a waterfall."

She sighed and followed him across the park.

It was a playground for the children of East Docks and the other town units surrounding it. Grass was interrupted by enough trees to climb on but not enough to keep a mother from seeing where her kid went.

Reflected sunlight poured through the gaps between the structures. The one overhead was painted light blue on the bottom with fluffy clouds for variation. Marcus traced the lines of the building. Each corner of the one above was supported by one of the lower structures.

"C'mon, I see an escalator." Alys pulled at Marcus' sleeve.

The escalator was farther away than she'd thought. The steps were square, wide enough for four strangers or many friends. A flat approach let them step on and adjust their position to be clear of the red stripes. It carried them along the corner of East Docks.

The pine forest painted on the building was more detailed than Marcus had realized. A cardinal sitting on a branch was taller than he was. He could distinguish individual feathers. *Was it all that detailed, or just where people could see?* he wondered.

At the top the view changed from the painted bottom to the true nature of the structure. It had an open frame, not painted walls. Shops declared themselves with bright paint. Throngs of people crowded the central aisles.

"It's a mall," said Alys. "Or a bazaar or something. Let's go see what they have."

Marcus hung back. "I'd rather come back when we know the place better. Crowds can be trouble."

He turned to study the level. A belt of trees lined the windows, making a gap between the outer wall of the arcology and the blocks holding the people. None of the other structures in sight had the open frame of the bazaar. They were solid walls like the ones below, painted with nature scenes. One had the crowded foliage and bright birds of a rainforest, the other an open savannah. Windows and balconies were painted to match the murals, sometimes invisible until they were at the right angle.

Marcus and Alys followed a walkway around the perimeter of the bazaar. The open side let them look down at the painted wall receding downward until they were walking over the park. Then another residential structure rose up to support the corner of the bazaar.

He looked up. The building supported by the bazaar wore a mackerel-scale cloud pattern on its base. In the gap between that structure and the next he saw interlocking stacks of them rising to the top of the city.

A local passed them towing a stack of boxes balanced on a floater. He nodded to the couple. Marcus returned it.

"Ardal, that's it," said Marcus.

"What?"

"The name of the interior structures," he said, waving at the one they were walking past. "That's what Wynny called them."

"Who's Wynny?" snapped Alys.

"The broker's daughter. She showed Tets and me around the first night. Sharp kid. Going to be a real wheeler-dealer when she takes over the business."

"Is she pretty?"

"I guess. Has the local look—oval face, long black hair."

Alys looked like she'd tasted something sour. "Might want to pull your history books out again. Lots of explorers got in trouble by being too friendly with the natives."

Marcus laughed. "It's not like that. Nobody's going to pay any attention to me when Tets is around. She even got to see him show off his muscles brawling."

She picked up her pace, leaving Marcus behind.

He stared at the braids wound on the back of her head, wondering what he'd said wrong.

Oh. I guess she is sweet on me. He'd wondered how serious her flirting was. Serious enough that being called a 'nobody' for paying attention to him offended her.

Marcus jogged to catch up with Alys. He grabbed her elbow, pulled her around to face him, and pressed his lips to hers. "Hey. My only interest in the natives is to find out what they'll buy so we can take a fortune home. Okay?"

"Okay." Alys gazed into his eyes, her hand resting on his bicep. A flush pinked her cheek.

As they started walking again Alys snuggled into his side, sliding her arm around his waist. Marcus put his arm over her shoulders.

He'd meant the kiss as an apology, but it seemed to mean more to her. He'd been trying not to let things go too far. His father's lectures on fraternization were sprinkled with stories of shipboard romances gone wrong. Marcus resolved to be more careful.

They stayed in the embrace as they went up the next escalator. The walkway around the third-level ardal widened out into a viewing platform a third of the way along the side.

Marcus walked to the edge of the platform. A glance around revealed its advantages. He could see through gaps in the array of ardals to a park on the bottom level of the city. Looking up in a different direction showed a gap among the higher ardals clear to the gridded dome covering the city.

There were only two more levels of ardals above them. The third level didn't have anything they hadn't seen below. They found the nearest escalator and went up.

The ardals were the usual solid truncated-pyramid blocks on this level. Nothing stood out as worth investigating. A line of trees against the transparent outer wall looked no different from the ones on the level below. The pair headed toward the next ardal over to take the escalator up.

As they approached it Marcus could hear a noise from the far side of the ardal. It was too steady to be a roar, too high-pitched to be a rumble. He steered Alys around the escalator and followed the sound.

From the walkway along the ardal Marcus couldn't see what was causing the noise. There was something past the ardal. He could see a shadow where normally sunlight would flow through the gap between structures.

The noise grew louder as they kept walking. At the corner of the ardal they couldn't hear each other speak. The source of the shadow was visible as a mass of trees.

Coming around the corner they could see the trees went to the outside wall. They were dense enough to keep anything from growing underneath them. The edge of the forest was set back from a lake. People clustered on the greensward along the shore.

Then they could see the source of the noise. The side of this ardal wasn't a painted nature scene. It was textured with rocks and ridges, diverting the cascade of water from the top until it spread to the whole width of the wall at the base. The wall cut back to make an overhang. The solid curtain of water fell into the lake with a steady thunder, white noise drowning any conversation below a shout.

Marcus and Alys stood, eyes drawn into the eddies and foam of the waterfall. When they moved again it was to slide along the lakeshore to find a better angle. They joined a crowd likewise mesmerized by the natural force of the water.

When Marcus turned from the waterfall he wasn't sure how long he'd been entranced. He studied the crowd around him. It was mixed. Locals, Censorials in uniform, and other spacers with a mix of clothing and faces.

The locals wandered more. Some were swimming in the lake. Brightly colored fish swam among the people. Other locals followed paths into the forest.

Alys shook herself. "Wow. That's something."

"Yep. Let's explore the woods a little then come back to the waterfall."

She agreed.

A hip-high barrel turned out to be an automated drink dispenser. Alys convinced it to charge the ship's account for a bottle of sea-grape juice. Marcus took another.

He examined the trees as they entered the forest. They weren't any species he'd seen on Fiera. Only a few broad leaves were scattered on the ground. Someone—or thing—must sweep it regularly.

The forest muffled the sound of the waterfall. The path took them past clearings, most filled with people singing or talking or just quietly drinking. The beverage barrels were at the edge of each cluster.

There'd been plenty of children by the lake, but the forest groups were adults, some mostly retirees. When Marcus saw one with a group of children at the center he drew closer to listen.

A storyteller was spinning a tale of adventure to a mixed group. The children sat on the ground before him, eyes wide. Their mothers were on folding chairs behind them. The outer ring was other adults who'd been caught by the story while passing by.

The storyteller had a Jaaphisii look. He wore a vest covered with pockets and his face had the burnt look Marcus had seen on the Jaaphisii at the docks. He was faded, though, as if he hadn't been to sea for years, and wrinkled with age.

Marcus thought he'd have a hard time as a sailor without legs. The storyteller's legs ended at midthigh. He sat on a float disk, hovering a couple of feet above the ground. His shorts were sewn shut, hiding whatever scars were still on the legs.

"The terrorfish swam so hard the rope almost pulled our boat under the water. The sea was sloshing over the sides. All four of us bailed as fast as we could." The storyteller mimed scooping and flinging water with a bucket. "Then it turned, pulled us so hard to port we all fell over. Worse, a second boat had a harpoon stuck in, and in the turn our boats smacked together. My boat's hull cracked. Seawater sprayed through the crack like a fan."

The children were rapt. Even the adults were paying close attention. The storyteller lifted a bottle from the edge of his float disk, drained the last of it, and held it up.

The mothers all traded looks, but none seemed to think it was their turn. The silence lengthened. Then one of the men standing in the outer ring went to the drink dispenser and produced another bottle of beer.

The storyteller took it and started talking before even opening the bottle. "There we were, terrorfish dragging us through the sea and a crack spraying water faster than we could bail. Looked like we'd be going down to feed the fishes instead of the other way around this time."

He took a swig of the beer. "So I pulled off my shirt, ripped it the long way, and stuffed it into the crack." Fingertips made pushing motions in a curve. "Made my mate give me his shirt to get the rest of it. We were still leaking, but we could keep up. The water was halfway to our knees."

The children all looked at where his knees weren't. The adults carefully didn't.

"As I bailed more I caught a glimpse of the other boat—empty. Four men gone. Never did find out what happened to them. My guess is they fell out when the boats knocked together."

The tale concluded with the terrorfish weakening as it bled from the harpoon wounds, more Jaaphisii ships catching up, and the beast brought into a city for sale.

"And then there was a party, but that's not a story for tender ears," said the storyteller.

Marcus said, "How about the story of how you lost your legs?"

A few of the mothers flinched. A twelve-year-old boy sat up hopefully.

"That's not a beer story, my spacer friend. That's a whiskey story."

Marcus turned to the drink dispenser. A few moments with its menu revealed the whiskey options. He flinched at the price but decided this was marketing, not entertainment, and he had the right to invest some money in it.

When the machine disgorged the whiskey, Marcus carried it over to the old man. His eyes widened. He gave Marcus a respectful nod as he took it.

Oh. He was expecting a glass, not a bottle.

"Well, my friend, I'm Kilrad. I'll tell your story. Might be a bit bloody for the younger ones."

Kilrad made a production of opening the bottle, providing time for mothers to drag their children away. The twelve-year-old insisted on staying. His mother settled back into her folding chair with a sigh.

Marcus sat in the space vacated by the little ones. Alys reluctantly joined him. One sip of the whiskey was enough to start the story.

"Anyone ever eat some kraken?" asked Kilrad.

That was what the Goch clan had served at the welcoming dinner. Marcus raised his hand, along with all the natives.

"You might think a kraken is an animal. It's not. It's a crew of animals. Each tentacle you see is a separate beast with its own eye, own brain, own beak."

He went on to describe a hunt. The Jaaphisii would show decoys to each side of the kraken to fool them into breaking their cooperation and working against each other.

"Then it was just a matter of binding it, tying up the tentacles so they couldn't untangle themselves and break free. I could hold my breath longer than anyone else in the fleet, so I was one of the men who volunteered to dive under dragging a rope. Once the tips were bound it was safe work."

Kilrad's throat caught on the last phrase. He lifted the bottle and drank down two swallows.

His audience was silent.

"Now, one member of this kraken was a youngster. Only a third the length of the others. It stuck the tip between a couple of others and grabbed my ankle."

The twelve-year-old put his hands over his face, peeking between the fingers.

"It yanked me up to the head. I saw the full circle of beaks opening and closing. I've asked other Jaaphisii fleets. No one but me ever saw that and lived."

A sip of whiskey.

"An adult beak would have swallowed me whole. But the youngster wanted to taste me itself. I kicked at the tongue hard enough it couldn't fit me in past the thighs."

Kilrad held his hands flat and swept them toward his stumps like a guillotine blade.

"It bit through my muscles as the beak closed but couldn't break the bones. Hurt more than anything. I didn't scream, though. You don't scream when you need every bit of air in your lungs."

Another sip.

"I passed out, don't know if it was from blood loss or running out of air or what. I woke as my mates were hauling me into a boat. They tied off my legs then went back to binding the kraken.

"When we set course for the nearest city the ship's barber took a look at me. Said I might live, but the flesh of the lower legs would not. So he took an axe to the bone just above the knee."

Kilrad mimed bones extending from his stumps. "I looked a fright when we reached port. The fleet donated a whole tentacle to pay for my care. The charity hospital did the rest for free. Now here I am."

Sip.

Marcus asked, "Did they regrow any of your legs?"

Kilrad laughed. One of the men listening said, "Spacer, he was in the charity hospital, not Top Level." That was illustrated with a wave at the ardal above them.

"Where did you get the floater from?" asked Marcus.

The audience started to drift away, bored by this topic. Kilrad looked after them but turned back to Marcus. "The hospital gave it to me. They wanted me able to earn my keep, you see."

"What do you do?"

"Night watchman. I'm scarier than alarms and harder to fool than the cameras." Kilrad's grin would scare a teenage vandal. "Good for fed and bed, but a man likes more than that."

Marcus nodded. "Thank you very much for your stories."

The audience was gone now. Kilrad hovered away, whiskey bottle held tenderly in his lap.

"I'm glad that's over," said Alys. "That was disgusting."

"But useful," said Marcus.

"How?"

He shook his head and led her away from the clearing with the drink dispenser. When he felt sure there were no people or machines to eavesdrop on them he said, "They can't regrow limbs here. Or at least it's really expensive. At home you could regrow ten or twenty limbs for the cost of an anti-grav car. One shrunk down to be a wheelchair?

Probably could regrow a hundred legs for that. That's our market. We need to bring medical gear. We'll make a fortune."

"Oh," said Alys, overwhelmed by the release of the excitement he'd been hiding.

"Let's get back to the ship. I have to tell the captain."

***

The fee for keeping *Azure Tarn* in a hangar for a day was reasonable. Demanding a one month stay was extortion. But Captain Landry bit his tongue and paid it. The next hurricane was closing in.

Some ships avoided storm and fee by going back up to orbit. The fuel cost was smaller than the hangar fee. Landry didn't want to do that. The Censorial officials in Bundoran hadn't noticed anything odd about *Azure Tarn*. The orbital traffic control crew might be more observant.

One advantage of the hangar was access to a basement level tram circuit connecting all the hangars to the city. That saved the crew from walking across the spaceport in their fancy clothes. They fit in a single open-topped tram car.

There were a few seats left over, reminders that Gander and Betty were assigned to the ship. Landry wasn't worried about security. If the Censorial government wanted to go through their ship it wouldn't sneak aboard. Those two were staying on the ship so they wouldn't start a fight with the Goch family.

Wynny Goch waited at the tram station. She was dressed for the party in a gown of shimmering purple. Once she'd been introduced to the rest of the crew she led them to Goch Home.

Crossing the park to the East Docks ardal they noticed the artificial lights were on despite it being an hour to sunset. The outer edge of the hurricane formed a thick cloud bank over the city. Streams of rainwater ran down the outer windows.

The main hall wasn't set up for dining this time. The center was cleared for dancing. Tables and chairs lined the edges. A band was setting up their instruments. Dancing lessons were being given to a couple dozen youngsters accompanied by recorded music.

Vychan and his wife Emlyn met them at the entrance. They led Lane and Niko Landry off for drinks while Wynny took the rest to the dance students. Niko sipped his wine cup warily, then took another sip with relief. This was a gentle white wine, not the confession-inducing brandy Vychan had served during his last visit.

When topping off Niko's glass Vychan whispered, "Do you have it?"

Niko twitched his hand toward his son. "He does."

"Good. Will your boy want a dance with Nia? It's her party."

"I'm sure he'd be honored to," answered Landry.

Emlyn laughed. "Being honored is not enough to force his way onto her list tonight. The dances are demanded not just by every scion who might make a match for her but also by those wanting to show their young men off to everyone in attendance."

"Has it become that bad?" asked Vychan.

His wife pointed toward a closed door. "In there Nia is fighting her mother to keep two boys she knows on the list lest her entire night be with strangers."

Lane said, "As proud as we are of Marcus, he can meet Nia another night."

"Thank you. Please forgive my unwise suggestion," said Vychan. "Oh, Captain, would you object to those tractor parts being melted down?"

"Not at all, if we get a decent price for them," said Landry.

"Good. I may have a buyer for the vanadium and niobium." Vychan described his latest calls among Bundoran's industrial clans.

On the dance floor the younger members of the crew were trying their best to learn the dances. Tets enjoyed flinging himself about to the music without bothering with the fancy footwork. Soon was at least a half beat behind. Welly tried to coach her.

The instructor paused in chanting the steps to study his new students. As Marcus skipped by he said, "Good enough."

Marcus smiled. He'd settle for that praise. Going through the figures without ruining it for anyone else was all he hoped for.

Next the instructor studied Alys. She held onto Marcus' hand and shuffled her feet to keep position. Rather than address her the instructor turned back to Marcus. "Help her as best you can, lad."

Alys improved a bit before the next batch of guests arrived. When that group came through the entrance the dance instructor shut down the music and urged all the students to the sides. The musicians stopped fiddling with instruments and gear, taking their seats.

A grandfatherly man strode to meet the new arrivals. Marcus recognized him as Garth Goch, Vychan's uncle. There were a few minutes of small talk. Garth walked back into the middle of the hall and waved to a teenage girl to join him.

She walked slowly across the dance floor, possibly scared of disturbing her coiffure. Black curls were stacked atop each other in a pile larger than her head. The dress was elaborate, shiny black fabric with silver ruffles, but not heavy enough to keep her from doing any of the dances Marcus had learned.

Garth put a hand on the girl's back, guiding her to stand before him facing the thickest part of the crowd. "Welcome, guests," he began, his voice filling the hall. "Thank you, friends, neighbors, and partners, for coming to my granddaughter Nia's outing day!"

Applause greeted this with a few cheers and whistles mixed in.

"From today Nia may travel without chaperone, sign contracts, and marry out of clan Goch." Garth went on to praise Nia's many fine qualities, including her school grades, bookkeeping she'd done for the family business, and efficient performance of her kitchen duties.

Alys leaned toward Marcus. "I thought this was a debutante party. He's giving a resumé for her."

He nodded. "Families are businesses here. To get a good marriage she has to convince them she'll contribute to the work. Or that she'll be a supervisor or something in Goch."

"These people are strange."

Marcus shrugged. "They'd probably think Fiera is nuts."

She turned towards him. "Is that why you're wearing your resumé?"

"It's the fanciest outfit I have." He tugged on the collar of his uniform jacket.

Captain Landry wore a blue dress uniform with enough gold braid to convince any passenger or inspector this was the man in charge. The first mate's version was slightly more subdued. As the ship's supercargo Marcus also had a uniform. His only bore a single gold braid on each cuff and epaulette. Gold buttons and piping drew the eye up to the stiff collar. He'd decorated the chest with pins the Professional Spacer Institute handed out for passing certification exams.

"And it's getting the locals to smile at you," she said.

"That's just the ones I met the first time I came here."

To Marcus' relief, Alys was distracted by the end of the speech. A visiting grandfather led a boy a year or two older than Nia out. After introductions, Garth waved to the band. The couple began dancing. Their patriarchs moved to the walls. Other couples moved out onto the floor.

This dance was an easy one. Marcus steered Alys through the turns. This one had no partner switches. The music was pleasant. Two singers sang nonsense words, being instruments instead of vocalists.

The next dance formed into long lines. The movements pulled Alys away from Marcus, but whichever way she turned there was someone whose movements she could copy.

Rather than attempt the third dance, Marcus led Alys to a table with a cauldron of some beverage. He cautiously tasted his cup before passing the second to Alys. Mixed fruit juice with just a hint of alcohol. Perfectly safe. He handed her the cup.

As she drank he said, "Want to let one of these boys dance with you?"

"Trying to ditch me?"

"It's a business event. We're supposed to mingle."

"I barely have their accent right. How can I handle a real conversation?"

"Make that your hook. Tell him you need help with pronunciation. Any guy would be happy to explain how to say it right."

"I'll bet," she said sourly.

"Marcus! Are you enjoying the party?" asked a twenty-something

Goch snagging a cup of the punch. He was a couple of inches shorter
than Marcus with a neat goatee.

"Very much, Dilwyn. I'd like you to meet my shipmate Alys."

Dilwyn cheerfully chatted up Alys. She held up her end of the
conversation and acquiesced to joining the next dance.

"Smoothly managed," said Wynny, stepping into the void.

Marcus answered, "She's a bit shy. Just needed a nudge."

"Of course." Without any nudge or request Marcus found himself
on the dance floor again. He reached out to Wynny's waiting hands and
they joined the other couples.

This one hadn't been covered in the lessons, but it was similar to
the waltz Marcus learned back on Fiera so he followed it well enough.

"Is your cousin enjoying her evening?" he asked. "She's been going
from partner to partner without a break."

"Oh, she'll have rests," said Wynny. "Her mother will make sure of
it. But this is work for Nia, not play." She tilted her head. "Which is it
for you?"

"Both. I'm learning about your world and your culture. And
enjoying meeting people." Marcus tried an experimental twirl, which
brought a giggle from her.

After the waltz, the music paused while the dancers sorted
themselves into circles of six.

Wynny poked at a pin on Marcus' chest. "Is that a shipping
container?"

"Yes. I'm a certified cargomaster."

She sniffed. "Everyone in the family learns to use a crane, but we
don't give them medals for it."

"Does a warehouse tip over and kill everyone inside if you put all
the containers on one side?"

"Um, no."

"It's more complicated on a spaceship."

Then the circle started spinning and there was no time to chat.

Niko Landry and Vychan Goch noticed their children dancing
together. Landry seized the chance to turn the conversation from
business. Complimenting Wynny's grace brought forth a description of

her abilities as a researcher and hard bargainer. It reminded him of the speech the Goch patriarch had made describing Nia.

Landry realized this hadn't stopped being a business conversation. He found himself laying out Marcus' education and certifications in response to Vychan's questions. *Should I be having this conversation?* he asked himself. *I'll be damned if I'll trade my son off as part of some deal.*

The PSI certifications impressed Vychan. "Is he qualified to command a ship, then?"

"Not yet." Landry nibbled on a fishball-on-a-stick. "He needs more time serving as a bridge officer. Right now he's working the hold mostly. I want him to qualify as a supercargo for larger ships in case he needs to get a job elsewhere."

Vychan refilled his punch cup. "So he can marry out?"

"Yes and no. Most of our businesses aren't families. But when he wants to marry it'll be easier if he's working a ship with a scheduled run instead of an irregular one where he'd rarely see home."

"His wife would not be on his ship?"

Landry cast a fond glance at Lane, immersed in a gaggle of matrons. "It's a rare woman who's willing to raise a family someplace as uncomfortable as a spaceship."

Vychan let out a mild harrumph. "No daughter or niece of mine would put her comfort over her husband's business."

"On Fiera, it's the children we try to make comfortable."

Landry tried to think of a way to change the subject. Vychan did it for him.

"This dance is ending," said the broker. "Let's meet them."

The two men moved through the groups chatting by the wall, meeting Wynny and Marcus as they arrived at the punch bowl. Vychan let the boy have one cup before saying, "It's time." He turned to Wynny. "If anyone asks, you're still dancing with him."

She nodded.

Vychan led the two Landrys toward the hall between the kitchen and the storage rooms. He talked up the virtues of a new wine he'd discovered.

Landry was puzzled. This hallway didn't go to Vychan's private office.

The door Vychan opened revealed a utility room. Pipes lined the ceiling and walls. A locker produced three garments. "Put these on," said Vychan, unfolding his own.

Marcus gave his father an inquiring look. Landry shrugged. *I don't know what's going on either.* They donned the ponchos.

Vychan tugged each one's hood until the edge was level with their noses. "From here on, make no noise until I say it's safe. Do you understand?"

Both Landrys nodded.

Vychan turned to a wall covered with pipes and conduits. A panel indistinguishable from the others popped out of position. He pushed it ahead of him as he passed through the hole, waving for the others to follow.

The ponchos would have made sense if this took them outside into the storm. Instead Landry found himself in an infrastructure volume. A massive I-beam sloped diagonally through it, supporting the upper layer of the archology. Cables and pipes travelled inside it. The whole collection was wrapped in a pipe, its interior lined with more pipes. A set of narrow steps followed the edge of the beam.

Vychan fit the panel back into place and started down the steps.

Landry followed, glancing back to make sure Marcus was staying with them. It was a good thing they were going down. That was the only direction he could see with the damn poncho on.

They continued down past the bottom of the ardal. This had to be basement or sub-basement level. Tunnels met at odd angles. Vychan chose branches without hesitation.

Going back to the party—or even the ship—was tempting Landry more and more. Whatever this was, it wasn't the simple trade of books he'd asked for. But it might already be too late to back out. Vychan would object if they turned around. An argument could attract cops. An arrest for trespassing could draw Censorial attention. Hell, Vychan could report them to the Censorate himself if he was pissed enough. Visitors from outside Censorial territory probably carried a bounty. No, whatever was going on, Landry would have to see it through.

The lower levels were noisier. Water rushed through pipes. Pumps thumped. Electrical motors hummed. Distant noises, impossible to separate, made a background buzz.

Then they were walking on bedrock. It was smooth enough to not trip on but the signs of construction machinery could still be seen in the grooves in the rock. Puddles glittered in the safety lights.

Tunnel became chamber. Thirty-foot steel tanks formed a circle. In the center stood a pumping station. The pipes connecting it to the tanks stood ten feet above the bedrock. Under them more than two dozen people were gathered. They turned to face the trio as they arrived. Everyone was in black ponchos, hoods covering their faces.

Vychan stopped ten yards from the pumping station. Landry stood on his right and felt Marcus come up on his other side.

The waiting people approached, spreading out in a semicircle around the trio. One stepped forward in the center.

Vychan bowed to him. "Nyrath, I bring friends wishing to trade knowledge."

Nyrath lifted his hood high enough to see the trio clearly, though his face was still shadowed. "What do they offer for trade?"

Marcus stepped forward at Vychan's wave. He lifted the poncho to reach his big thigh pocket. His palms were slippery with sweat. He needed both hands to hold up the digital book.

"This is the textbook for my history class. It's called *The History of Humanity*. It covers history from the beginning to when my ancestors fled from a war into the Fieran Bubble, and the nine-hundred-some years since then."

"The beginning?" Nyrath's voice cut through the whispers of the others. "Where does it begin?"

"On Earth. When true humans separated from the other hominoid species. It's just an overview of that period. The Paleolithic and Neolithic only get a chapter each."

Nyrath stepped forward, hands reaching out for the book. "This history is continuous? No gaps?"

"It only discusses the major events. But it has the whole timeline from pre-history to a constitutional crisis forty years ago."

One poncho-clad figure dropped to his knees. Another swayed, was grabbed by the men beside him, and was lowered to the bedrock.

Nyrath walked forward. Marcus met him halfway, placing the book in his hands.

"To think I let you in my house," muttered Vychan.

Landry asked, "What's the matter?"

"The things we don't know that we don't know. My friend, do you have any idea what would happen if the Censorate discovered that book?"

"They'd confiscate it?"

Nyrath quickly learned the interface to the book with Marcus' help and began exploring the contents.

The broker burst into laughter. "They'd kill all of us. Kill your crew and melt your ship into slag. Kill Clan Goch and all our party guests. Burn the ardal. Investigate everyone we talked to. Without saying why."

"Oh." Now Landry wanted to run back to the party, grab his crew, and take off from this horrible planet tonight.

Except *Azure Tarn* wasn't maneuverable enough to fly through a hurricane. They might not get clear of the hangar.

"Fortunately for us all the Censorate is too complacent to go around checking," said Vychan. "But if they were to hear a hint of this book's existence . . ."

"Damn." That wasn't enough to relieve Landry's feelings, but what could?

Nyrath found how to reset the timeline reference from the Fieran calendar to any of sixteen alternatives. He turned to face the others. "My brothers and sisters in truth. By the Gregorian calendar it is now the year 3756."

The announcement drove some back in shock. One struck her head on a pumping station valve. Others bellowed laughter. The man at the right end of the semicircle cried, "Million year Censorate my sopping wet arse!"

Marcus retreated back to his father.

Nyrath turned to the Landrys. "My friends. We accept what you offer. And we shall repay you with anything in our power. Our secret knowledge, our wealth, our lives, our families. What you wish shall be yours."

A scene from a movie flashed into Landry's mind. A conqueror demanding the natives fill a room with gold to the height of his head. A full hold of gold jewelry would make this a profitable trip.

And make Censorial Customs wonder what the other side of the deal was. No. He needed to keep a low profile.

Landry's throat caught his first attempt to answer. He coughed, and said, "Thank you. We'd like to see what you have of your history. But what we need most is for this to stay secret. My crew did not intend to risk execution by coming here."

"The Censorate executes people for far less truth than this," said Nyrath dryly. "My brothers and sisters will keep the secrets safe."

The man at the end of the line blurted, "Where did you come from that you don't fear holding a history book?"

Landry sighed. "We're from Fiera. It was trapped in a hyperspace bubble. The shoals finally shifted enough to make a hole. We're the first ship through. We didn't know anything about your Censorate."

"That, Brother Afan, is something we did not need to know," said Nyrath sternly. "We shall all hold it more closely than the existence of the book."

Afan demanded, "Have you come here to free us from the Censorate?"

"No, no," said Landry. "We're merchants. We came here to trade. We didn't know your Censorate existed."

Marcus stepped forward. "Once we're back home we'll tell everyone about it. I'm sure they'll want to help."

Landry grabbed his son's shoulder and squeezed hard. "We cannot speak for our government. We don't know what they'll do."

Whispers among the others became full voiced conversations. When a couple started shouting, Nyrath broke in again.

"Brothers and sisters, we must not speculate. Our business is facts. Truth. Not guesses or hunches. Brother Vychan may give our new friends copies of the history he has. All of us shall give what favors we can. Now we shall disperse. Do not go home until you have calmed."

Vychan hustled his guests away before anyone else could buttonhole them.

Glancing back Landry saw the group break into loud conversations.

The ponchos were more of a problem going upstairs. Landry held the front of it up so he wouldn't trip on it. He pulled the hood back so he could see more than Vychan's feet ahead of him.

Rushing water was louder in the pipes. Was that normal, or was the hurricane causing leaks? He decided to ask Vychan once they could talk safely.

Marcus let out a half-voiced "sorry" as he bumped into his father.

Landry didn't waste breath on a response. Naturally the boy wasn't slowing down. The older ones were feeling the climb. Landry knew he wasn't keeping up the pace he had. Even so he sometimes had to pause not to run into Vychan.

The poncho made the exercise heat him up even more. He felt cool air on his face and around his ankles. The rest of him was sweating. One advantage of the fancy uniform. It was thick enough to hide sweat stains.

Before he had to worry about heat stroke, they reached the secret door into Goch Home. Vychan popped out the panel, hurried them through, and replaced it.

The ponchos went back into their locker. A water bottle was passed around.

"Right," said Vychan. "Let's go back in and hope no one missed us."

The hallway was empty until they reached the kitchen. Wynny emerged and swept Marcus away. They reached the dance floor as another of the waltz-like dances began.

"Perfect," she said. "Stay to the outside where we'll be seen."

He took her hand, put his other on her waist, and began moving to the music.

Wynny slid close. "You're holding me as if it's our third dance," she whispered. "It's our eleventh. Act it."

She pressed her thigh against his and leaned against his chest.

Marcus gulped. When she let go of his hand he slid his arms

around her back. She matched the embrace firmly.

"Better."

Her ear was just below his mouth. Very quietly Marcus said, "So you know?"

"Only that everyone should think you've been dancing with me all night." Wynny lifted her head, stared at his eyes, and leaned into him again. "I think I'm happier this way."

They made it three quarters of the way around the dance floor before the music stopped. Marcus promptly led Wynny to the nearest punchbowl. His throat was still parched from the climb up from bedrock.

As he finished the first cup Alys appeared on his left. "Dance, sir?" she said with a bright smile.

Wynny stepped back and nodded.

Marcus went to the dance floor with Alys, keeping up with her brisk pace so he wouldn't be dragged. They took a place in one of the circles of eight forming up.

"Where the hell have you been?" whispered Alys as the circle moved left.

Marcus protested, "It's not what you think."

Then the woman on his other side took his hand and they twirled two rotations before returning to their partners.

"I know it's not what I thought," hissed Alys. "I found her helping her grandmother in the kitchen."

The circle squeezed to the center and went out again.

"It was business."

"So, tell me. I work in the business."

Now they circled to the right.

"You don't need to know."

"Don't be telling me that. I'm part of the crew."

He embraced her for a tight spin.

"I am the supercargo."

"Oh, you're playing the officer card now?"

"Yes. Stop asking. That's an order."

Marcus released her as the spin ended. Alys turned and ran from the dance floor.

The other woman seized his hand, pulling him into the twirl. As he came around he could see the man on the other side glaring at Marcus as if it was his fault the man had no one to twirl.

It probably was.

As the twirl ended, a plump matron hurried into Alys' empty spot, taking Marcus' hand as the circle moved left.

"Thank you. Sorry," he said.

She smiled. "Happy to sneak my way into a dance. I'd never have one with a handsome boy like you."

Next, he embraced her for a spin. She moved more easily than Alys despite her age.

"Don't feel bad about it, boy," she whispered. "It's better to find out she's like that before you marry her."

Marcus mumbled a polite acknowledgement and focused on the dance.

When he stumbled off the dance floor, Wynny waited with a cup of punch.

"Did you see . . . that?" Marcus said once he'd downed it.

"Oh, yes. Father will be thrilled."

"Huh? Why?"

"There's nothing like a jealous girlfriend throwing a fit to convince people we actually were dancing together all night."

"She's not my girlfriend."

"Don't tell me. Tell her." Then Wynny had mercy on him and found him a seat by the munchies table.

Two plates of high protein snacks and plenty of drinks restored Marcus to where he wanted to dance again. Alys pretended not to hear when he asked her to dance. He wound up on the floor with a series of Goch cousins, and a couple of guests who were curious about the spacer.

When the party broke up, the crew shuffled back to the train station. Alys sulked but it wasn't mentioned with Soon, Roger, Welly, and Tets all competing over who'd enjoyed the party the most. The closest to a negative comment from them was when Tets said, "Dilwyn could recite his Goch ancestors back for six generations. Made a song of it. But he can't write it down. Says that's illegal. This place is strange."

"It is different," agreed Captain Landry.

At the station, Landry pulled his son aside. "We'll take the next one," he told the rest.

When the tram pulled away, the station was just an empty concrete box. The open top let them hear the hurricane beating at the clear walls of the city.

Marcus fidgeted as he waited.

"Do you remember why I left Betty and Gander on the ship?" asked the captain.

"You didn't want them pissing off the natives."

"My exact words?"

Marcus had to think. He hadn't been paying close attention. "You didn't want someone starting a war by being rude to a VIP."

"That's right." His father leaned in. "I also don't want someone starting a war by convincing an anti-Censorial secret society to launch a rebellion because we'd have their backs."

The young man wilted under the glare. "I'm sorry. It just burst out."

The captain kept glaring.

"Don't we want to help these people?" asked Marcus.

Captain Landry rubbed his face with both hands. "How many inhabited worlds are in the Fieran Bubble?"

"Three. If you count Svalbard."

The joke fell flat.

"How many in the Censorate?"

"Um . . . I don't know."

"Nobody does. Starmaps are forbidden, there are no books about other worlds, they don't even teach how many planets are in this system in the schools."

Marcus said, "It could be hiding that there's very few."

"No. Vychan's met ships from fourteen other worlds. There're no barriers for incoming traffic. The Censorate is big enough that nobody has reached here from outside."

"Except us."

"Except us. And we're getting away with it because nobody's checking whether we're from outside."

"So there could be dozens of worlds in the Censorate."

"Or hundreds. Or thousands. With who knows how powerful a fleet and the industrial capacity to outbuild us by orders of magnitude. If we get into a war with the Censorate, they could stomp us flat."

"Oh."

The hurricane roared in the distance.

Landry said, "I like these people, I do. I think their situation sucks. But let's not get them killed."

Two drunken spacers stumbled down the stairs. They tried to sing a song together, getting stuck in the middle of each verse and restarting the refrain.

An empty tram pulled into the station. The Landrys and the drunks climbed aboard.

Marcus eyed the spacers and stayed quiet. His father took advantage of the silence to plan his lecture to the rest of the crew on the need to never mention any history to the locals.

***

As usual, Vychan wanted to meet in the spaceport tavern. Landry understood the logic of it. Strangers visiting Goch Home caused gossip among the neighbors. Too many visits by Vychan to *Azure Tarn* would cause suspicion among the Censorial authorities. The tavern was a safe rendezvous.

But not a comfortable one. Landry sat alone at a table in the corner. A dozen other spacers stood by the bar, trading stories and jokes. The Fieran wasn't welcome. He made sure he was far enough away he couldn't be suspected of eavesdropping.

With written or electronic star maps forbidden to civilians, the only way to find a new route was learn it from someone who'd been there. Following another ship was dangerous. Losing sight of the other in a cloud bank could lead to being lost forever in hyperspace.

Having a navigator who'd been there was safest. But there was a shortage of spacers willing to abandon their current ship for a one-way trip with a stranger.

Which left having someone else describe the route in enough detail for the listener to follow it on their own. Three spacers at a table were doing that now, judging by the hand gestures. Every spacer in the tavern would eventually be describing how to reach some planet. All other banter among them was subordinate to trading hyperspace routes.

The initial warm welcome they'd offered Landry went cold when he refused to tell them the way to Fiera. If he wouldn't trade, they didn't want to talk to him. If he was close enough to overhear, he'd get dirty looks.

Hence, corner table.

Vychan came through the door and scurried to the corner, flagging down a barmaid on the way.

"My apologies," said the broker. "I saw Maxen on the slideway and buttonholed him. His family handles used equipment sales. I can get some cheap floaters from him. Doesn't want any of your cargo, but he's open to a triangle trade."

"That's good news. Thank you."

The barmaid arrived with a pitcher of beer and two plates. Today's special was fish fried in batter with fried kelp chips. Conversation paused while they ate. The tavern food was delicious, as long as you didn't let it get cold.

Vychan swallowed his last bite. "How much used gear are you willing to take? I don't want to fill your hold with cast-offs."

"If they're functional cast-offs I'll take them. Cosmetic damage doesn't bother me. We can fix that on Fiera. Same for structure and controls."

"So you just want the antigrav units. What about spare parts?"

"I'll take some. Still want mostly working vehicles so we know how to assemble the parts." Landry chased the last of his chips with some beer.

"That gives me more flexibility. Which I need. This isn't going to be a simple triangular trade. I'm going to have more than one swap separating the receivers of your cargo from the ones providing what you want."

Landry topped off their mugs from the pitcher. "I'm sure you have reasons for doing it that way. But . . . wouldn't it be simpler to just auction off my cargo and pay cash for the floaters?"

"Ah. I haven't explained the excess profits tax." Saying the words put a sour expression on Vychan's face.

"No. But it does sound important."

"Normal tax rates apply on profits after expenses up to ten percent over what the Censorate thinks the goods are worth. Anything over that is taxed on a sliding scale. An open ended auction would cost you your ship if the bidding got high enough."

"What they think it's worth."

"Uh-huh. And if it's not in the book of valuation, they launch an investigation to see what the fair price is. Including a visit to the factory that made it to check production costs."

Now Landry wore a sour expression. "Yes, we want to avoid that."

"Barter isn't taxed. I may have to put cash in to grease some of the swaps, we'll pay taxes on that. But if it's small we won't face a Censorial audit."

Before Landry could reply, they were interrupted.

"Vychan! It's good to see a friendly face here," said a stranger. A second one echoed the sentiment.

The broker stood to embrace the new arrivals. "Jarnton! Mephora! Wonderful! When did you land?"

Landry didn't say anything. He focused on holding his jaw still so it wouldn't rudely drop open. These strangers were astonishing.

The various refugees settling the Fieran Bubble included representatives of every ethnic group, some unknown on Earth. There'd been some blending over the centuries, but most had at least a few almost pure descendants. Landry had met people who could pose as history book illustrations for "Scandinavian" and "West African."

The individual in front of him ('Jarnton' was what Vychan had called him), bore *both* skin colors. The eyes were a rich dark brown, almost black, set in skin the same color. The forehead above them was white, so pale that blood vessels made hints of red and blue against the skin. The colors alternated in horizontal stripes down the body, peeking out between the sides of an open vest. Many-pocketed shorts hid some of the skin, but the stripes were visible below where the shorts ended at the knees.

Landry looked back up at Jarnton's hair. The scalp stripes ran vertically back from the hairline. Tight brown curls stood next to yellow hairs standing in a spiky array.

"My friends, let me introduce you to my friend Captain Niko Landry," said Vychan. "It's his first visit here."

Jarnton shook Landry's hands with both of his, accompanying it with a warm smile. Mephora, standing too far back to reach, waved to acknowledge her introduction.

Vychan stole chairs from another table and summoned a pitcher of beer. Landry tried to keep from staring by switching his focus to whoever was talking. That neglected Mephora, who sat quietly on the other side of the table.

A pale stripe went across her icy blue eyes. The stripes were roughly the same as Jarnton's, offset by a few inches. At least on the head. Mephora wore a grey jumpsuit only revealing her hands and head. The hands were striped too.

"Fiera? I never heard of that one before," said Jarnton. "So how do you get there, and what are they buying?"

"I'm sorry, I can't say," said Landry.

"Really, he can't," echoed Vychan. "It's complicated. If we can ever tell the story I'll explain it to you then."

Mephora snorted in disbelief.

A wry grin spread over Jarnton's face. "I'm sure that's a fascinating tale." He turned the conversation to market conditions on Corwynt. His ship had a mixed cargo, most of which would be traded on other worlds.

When they began trading rumors of other planet' needs, Landry couldn't control his curiosity any more.

"Please forgive me if this is a rude question," he said. "And there's no obligation to answer it. But . . . how did you get those stripes?"

Jarnton chuckled. Mephora snarled, "Burnt if I want to hear any politics," and carried her beer over to a table of spacers.

"I'm sorry," started Landry.

Jarnton shook his head. "I'm not offended. She's just tired of hearing me go on."

He stretched out his arm, rotating it to show the stripes circling around. The brown stripes faded to tan in the palm of the hand. "Why are we zebras? Nobody knows. It's history." He said the word as if it meant mystery.

Jarnton continued. "It's genetics. We breed true with each other. If a zebra marries a monochrome, they'll have monochrome kids."

"All different shades," interjected Vychan.

"Yes, monochromes get so worked up about that. We also lack many hereditary diseases. So we're certain it was done on purpose. Why?" He shrugged.

"There's two theories, and two parties to go with them. One says this is a punishment, to warn everyone who sees us what horrible people we are. The other is that we were such good people this was a reward."

"Parties?" asked Landry.

Vychan explained, "Instead of appointing them all, the Censorate lets the zebras pick some local officials. People choose candidates, and whichever candidate has the most supporters gets the job."

"That way the Censies can blame one of us when a riot breaks out," quipped Jarnton. "Anyway, the theories drive our politics. The Peace party passes detailed laws, enforces them rigidly, and inflicts harsh punishments. Then the Joy party wins an election. They repeal some laws, ignore others, and turn loose the prisoners."

"There's some people begging the Censorate to let us do that here," said Vychan. "I'm not sure about it. Can you imagine the Jaaphisii picking the city administrators?"

"We don't let everyone vote. And you'll have to excuse me. My captain wants me to talk shifting hyperspace routes with someone. Well

met, Captain Landry. I hope to hear about your world someday."
Jarnton gave Vychan a hug and headed for the bar.

"Interesting friends you have," said Landry.

"I get to meet most off-worlders who come here. The zebras are more entertaining than most."

***

Marcus gently reeled out the crane's cable. The crate held on the end landed in the back of the flatbed floater Wynny Goch had backed into *Azure Tarn's* cargo hold. He let out a little more slack as the floater dipped under the weight. Then it came back up. He stopped the reel. "Ready to unhook," he called.

The floater swayed again as Alys climbed into the bed to disconnect the harness from the crate. That was the fourth and last. When she waved Marcus retracted the crane to its rest position and left the booth.

Wynny popped open the doors to the flatbed's cab. "Coming?"

"Just a moment," he answered. "Close the hatch behind us and you can have the rest of the day off," he said to Alys.

She nodded.

He belted himself into the floater.

"Relax," said Wynny. "I'm not going to throw you around. Some of the cargo might be fragile."

"If anything's fragile we probably broke it already," said Marcus. "There were some rough moments on the trip." That led to him describing the hyperspace storm they'd run into on their way to Corwynt.

"So that's why the hurricanes don't scare you," said Wynny.

"Oh, there's hurricanes on Fiera. We just get a few a year instead of having them all the time."

"Quiet planet."

The weather was calm over Bundoran. The hatch to the warehouse district tunnel stood open. She drove in and went to the smallest of the Goch clan's warehouses. The door answered her remote. She parked the flatbed in the far corner, behind a stack of barrels.

"Let's get this off. Can you handle that?" She waved at a forklift by the wall.

"Sure." At least, he didn't think it would be that different from the ones back home. The driving controls were the same. He stopped short of the floater to lift the forks, which let him try all the levers to find the right one without scraping the paint. Wynny had the back gate of the flatbed lowered. He scooped up a crate on the first try.

Marcus suppressed a smile. He figured he should look like he'd done that before.

The first two crates went next to the barrels. The other two were too far for the forklift to reach. He climbed onto the floater and started shoving them to the rear.

Wynny shook her head and climbed back into the cab. "You like doing things the hard way."

As he pushed on a crate the floater tilted up. Now he was pushing downhill, and had to stop before he sent it off the gate. "Yeah, that helps."

By the time he placed the fourth crate in a row with the others Wynny had brought up some empty bins about the same size as the crates. "Do you really not know what's in these?"

The crates were all labeled 'MISC CHILDRENS TOYS' in black letters. "We bought them cheap to top off the load," said Marcus. "I figure it's basic teddy bears and such."

"Let's find out." She handed him a prybar.

The first was used toys. Bears and other stuffed animals with a bit of wear. Balls with scrapes. Skateboards, ditto. Leather gloves (which led to the discovery that baseball didn't exist on Corwynt). Dolls of various types.

Wynny held up a plastic goblin. "What the heck is this?"

"It's the villain from a children's show."

"Hmmm. Won't sell unless we have the show."

"I'll add it to our list for the next trip."

That produced a grin. Wynny tossed the goblin into a bin and reached into the crate again. This time she pulled out a book with thick toddler-proof pages. "The Story of Chanukah," she read. She opened it to the title page. A second later she flung it away. The book bounced off the stacked barrels and skittered across the floor.

"What are you doing?" she snarled. "That's grounds for execution."

"Huh?" Marcus was too startled to respond intelligently.

"That's—that's a copy of a book from Earth!"

He retrieved the book and looked at the copyright notice. "Reprinted in 7474 from the 5792 edition. Um, I don't know what the current year is on that calendar, but that many years ago, it's from Earth, yes."

Wynny crossed her arms. "You are from outside the Censorate. I thought so."

"I'm—well—yeah."

"If a Censorial agent found that book we'd be executed."

"Oh. We'd better give it to your father to hide then."

That made her grin. "Ah, he's in a history society."

"Oh, crap. That was a secret, wasn't it?"

Wynny shrugged. "I knew he was in some secret society. He keeps disappearing without good reasons. I'm glad it's history."

"There's other kinds of secret societies?"

"Oodles. History, storytellers, people praying to the Sacrificed God." Her expression tightened. "And, rumor has it, circles of men who discuss the latest Censorial crime and draw lots to see who assassinates a Censy to pay for it."

"Ah."

"But Da's too sensible to be one of the last kind. Still, we need to get this book out of here. Along with any others that might be hiding." Wynny glanced in the open crate to check for more books then pried open the next. "What the heck is this?"

"It's for drawing on." Marcus demonstrated a few lines, then shook the gadget to erase it.

"Fine. Might be worth a credit. Not worth executing us for."

As more toys went into the bins without books turning up Wynny relaxed. She hid *The Story of Chanukah* behind a ventilation duct.

"So why did you come here?" she asked.

"Money," answered Marcus.

She snorted in disbelief. "You're risking execution for that?"

"We didn't know the Censorate existed. Our system has been isolated for nine hundred years. Long enough for the language to drift apart. For all we knew everyone was dead out here."

"Not much money in dead people."

"Our mechanic was all for looting ruins. I guess it's my father who wanted the money. I wanted to see what's out here. Others wanted adventure. And Betty hated the idea but we outvoted her so she was stuck."

This crate was mostly teddy bears. He tossed them into a bin in a steady stream as he spoke.

"So what do you think now that you found us?"

"I want to tear your fucking Censorate apart and bury the Censor in the ruins. As soon as I figure out how." He finished that with a grin at his own hubris.

She laughed. "I won't object. Just try to not get buried yourself."

***

The spaceport tavern was near empty with the lunch rush gone. Vychan explained the deal he'd made with the customer for the tractor parts. "They said they could deliver four more grav sleds but wouldn't have them until the ninth. Can you wait that long?"

"Certainly," said Captain Landry. "I'll take all the floaters I can get."

"Good." The broker made some notes on his tablet. "Oh, Mourning Day is almost here. Do you have your outfits?"

"What's—"

Vychan flung up a hand to cut off the question. He looked around the tavern. The nearby tables were empty. None of the staff or remaining patrons were paying attention to them. But it was still a bad idea to reveal Landry's ignorance of Censorial traditions.

"Do you have pure black clothes for every member of your crew?"

The captain shook his head.

"You're spacers, it doesn't have to be fancy. Send me a message with everyone's sizes and I'll find outfits. I'll bring them to the ship tomorrow."

"Thank you."

"Just taking care of my friends." The broker scooped up his tablet and left.

***

The actual delivery was made by Dilwyn Goch. Ten unlabeled black bags held all black clothes.

"What's with the big socks?" asked Soon. She held up a foot-shaped object, too loose to fit comfortably on skin.

"If you don't have black shoes you pull that over them," explained Dilwyn. "It'll keep you from being written down by some Censorial."

Tets shoved his shirt back in the bag. "I'd rather skip the whole thing."

"You can't do that!" Dilwyn's eyes widened in shock. "The Censorials check everyone's thumb. I was throwing-up sick once and my parents still dragged me out for it. They'll give people shocks for laughing or falling asleep. If you don't show at all—" He shuddered.

***

On the day, only half the usual number of ships were in port. Landry wondered if being off-planet was an acceptable excuse or if there'd be make-up sessions.

A Censorial officer visited *Azure Tarn* on the eve to provide exact times and places. The crew promised to obey.

In the morning they set out a little early. The tram station let them out into a stream of people going into the park. A line of posts held thumb-readers, minimizing the wait. A native police officer watched.

The crew huddled together in the vast crowd. The park was being filled shoulder to shoulder. Landry hoped it would be a calm event. If a stampede broke out, there'd be thousands hurt and no way to escape.

A hologram globe hovered over the middle of the park. It twisted slowly around to make all sides visible while turning on its axis.

"What is that?" asked Roger.

After a moment, Marcus whispered, "It's Earth. Earth without the oceans. See, there's where South America meets Antarctica. And now Africa's coming into view. That crater's different though."

All the Fierans had taken a year of Earth history in school. They could recognize the continents even if they weren't used to seeing the continental shelves around them. The crater in the corner of Africa made them twitch.

The globe kept turning. India was easily recognized. It had two craters. Tibet was unaltered. The east coast of Asia bore four craters. Landry looked away.

Censorial officials were scattered among the crowd, on floating disks that held them at shoulder height. Presumably they were the ones who'd administer punishment to anyone not showing the proper attitude.

A platform stood at one edge of the park. A few rows of people sat on it. Their clothes were visibly elaborate despite being pure black. Landry noticed many in the crowd wore tailored outfits. He felt underdressed in his pajama-like clothes. Which was silly if he'd never need to wear them again.

A Censorial officer in the normal dress uniform walked to the front of the platform. Projectors cast his voice over the crowd. Landry hid a smile. It was Koing, the same officious subaltern who'd inspected *Azure Tarn.*

"My fellow subjects of Censor Longinus. We gather today to mourn and remember the people of Earth. Planet Earth had peace and prosperity as part of the Censorate. They received protection and order. The people raised their children knowing the next generation would enjoy the same happiness their parents did."

The Censorial's tone went cold. "This was not enough for some Earthers. Their greed for power inspired them to revolt. The conspirators recruited others who loved to harm people by giving them an excuse to wield violence in their cause. Innocents who stumbled across their secrets were murdered, or forced into silence by threats to their children.

"Then the conspiracy struck. In a single day they murdered the hard-working administrators who kept Earth in order. Any Earthers who objected to the slaughter were killed as well to cow the population. Earth shivered in fear as the conspirators set up their blood-covered thrones."

Sounds of shock and horror came from the crowd. Landry dismissed them as fake, then wondered why he'd reacted so strongly. A few more reactions let him realize the reason. The gasps were synchronized, as if they were prayer responses in church.

"The only Censorial official left to fight back was the local naval commander, Commodore Wenliang. He gathered all available ground troops and launched a counter-attack. He hoped he could free the administrators awaiting execution. But the revolt had suborned factories to make heavy weapons. Despite their bravery, the Censorial Dragoons were overwhelmed by wave after wave of artillery fire. The supporting Navy ships were badly damaged by missiles and forced to withdraw.

"As they left they saw warships under construction to spread the revolt to other systems.

"Commodore Wenliang tried precision attacks from space next, losing more good men and ships to the secret weapons of the revolt. That left only one way to free Earth from the conspirators. Wenliang's ships found asteroids and pushed them into trajectories for Earth. Each was targeted on one of the leaders of the revolt.

"Once the rocks were falling toward Earth, Wenliang took his squadron back to the planet. His ships surrounded the world outside the range of the missiles. They broadcast the news of the asteroids."

The Censorial officer's voice shifted again. Instead of projecting the emotions of the story it became a dry lecturer's recitation.

"All subjects have the duty to serve the Censor. In normal times, this duty is to pay taxes and obey the law. In an emergency all may have to serve to repair damage and tend the injured. When a catastrophe strikes, duty will demand more."

Anger flowed into his voice. "The people of Earth failed in their duty. They were required to fight back against the conspirators. Suppress the revolt. Some did. If more had, there would be a happy ending to this tale. But most did nothing. They ignored Commodore Wenliang's pleas for action. They bowed in fear to the conspirators. And they paid the price."

More synchronized gasps greeted this.

"The Earthers did nothing. Commodore Wenliang could do nothing in response. The rocks fell."

The hologram overhead brightened. The craters glowed red and yellow as if they'd just formed.

"A population of billions. Too lazy or scared to do their duty. Unwilling to take down a conspiracy of less than a million. They failed in their duty to the Censor. Willfully failing the Censor is treason. The penalty for treason is death."

Marcus muttered, "This isn't mourning. It's gloating."

Landry grabbed his son's shoulder. "Shut up." He hissed into his ear, "Are you trying to get us all shot?"

"Let us mourn the cowardice of Earth," continued the Censorial. "Let us mourn the lost future of Earth. Let us mourn the plants and animals lost forever because humans failed to enjoy peace and order. Let us mourn the children of traitors, not responsible for the disaster around them."

Now the prayer responses were sobs and weeping. Landry looked around. He didn't see any tears.

The officer shifted from history to current times. He praised the people of Corwynt for doing their duty. Taxes were paid. Crime was low. People volunteered for Censorial service on other worlds. Disasters brought out volunteers.

That part of the speech was repeated with extra details for the city of Bundoran. Then specific people—all natives—were praised for exemplary performance of their duty. They were the ones seated on the platform behind the officer. Each one stood for their mention.

Landry clapped with the rest of the crowd for each name. He

glared at any member of the crew inclined to rest his or her hands.

When the last honoree sat, the hologram of ruined Earth became a man's head. He looked sixtyish. The expression was stern yet just. Landry couldn't match the face to any ethnic group found in the Fieran Bubble. Probably a new group hybridized from mixing all the others.

"Hail Censor Longinus!" cried the officer.

Landry echoed it with the crowd. There were two repeats. And then, thank God, they were done.

He expected a surge for the exits. Instead people stood around chatting. Maybe leaving too quickly was a sign of a Bad Attitude. Even if it was, he wanted out.

Picking their way through the crowd wasn't hard. From overheard conversations it seemed many locals were catching up with rarely seen acquaintances from other clans.

The seat on the tram car was much softer than it had felt on the way out.

***

The crew were silent on the tram ride, and walking to their ship, and even going up the ladder to the upper deck. The captain and first mate retired to their cabin. The chief engineer went to the engine room. The younger members of the crew gathered in the galley.

Tets spoke first. "Can you believe that shit!"

"I don't know. The Censorate has enough control over information to get away with faking it." Marcus was taking the question literally. "It could be fiction. It could have happened to another world. I just can't think of a reason to say it was Earth instead of some world nobody ever heard of."

Soon shivered. "It makes a difference. Destroying that history, where our ancestors were from, every plant and animal terraformers didn't take off-world . . . that's worse than some random colony."

"Who cares why?" demanded Betty. "Let's lift off and get the hell home before they execute us."

"That's up to the captain," snapped Roger.

"I'm not talking mutiny. I just want to get out of here."

"So do I," said Alys. She'd put a kettle on to boil. "But we need to finish trading first."

"Do we?" asked Welly. "We have all that metal. Isn't that enough profit?"

They all looked to Marcus. "We're not just getting money in the trades. These people have improved anti-grav technology. Or maybe we lost some tech when the Bubble was settled. Either way we need to bring some home, so we can figure out how to duplicate it."

Roger thought about that. "You're not just looking for a profit. That's to help the Bubble against the Censorate."

Marcus nodded. "We're going to have to face the Censorate sooner or later. Best to get all the advantages we can find."

Alys set tea cups out on the counter. "Can't we just hide? If they don't know we exist, they won't bother us."

Soon shook her head. "The inlet in the shoals is widening. If the Censorate sends a survey out, they'll find it. And find us."

"That only matters if they don't execute us first," snarled Betty.

Welly started at that. "Wait, why would they kill us? We haven't done anything."

"Some of our cargo is prohibited in the Censorate," said Marcus. "Plus, they might consider us spies."

"I guess we are spying on them," said Roger.

Tets threw his hands in the air. "Nice to know I'll deserve to be shot when it happens."

"We need to spy on them," said Soon. "Maybe not sneaking around spying but finding out everything we can. The Censorate is dangerous. We have to be prepared."

Welly snapped, "Prepared to what? Fight? Then Fiera is an airless rock covered in craters. Don't be stupid. Life's not so bad here. Why not go along with them?"

"Give up Shakespeare?" cried Roger. "Give up our history?"

"Is that worth having our planet destroyed? The people here are happy. There're no beggars on the street. Nobody dies alone in their house, unnoticed until the smell bothers the neighborhood." Welly wiped her eyes.

Marcus spoke firmly. "I think that's the culture on Corwynt, not the Censorate. But it doesn't matter if you're willing to surrender. There'd never be support in the Bubble for joining the Censorate. We're too stubborn."

"Damn straight," said Tets. "My grandpa still goes on about fighting in the Sweetmeat War and the Apprehension wasn't nearly as bad as this Censorate."

Betty muttered, "Yeah, that was a nasty war. Makes me wonder if the Bubble can cooperate enough to fight the Censorate."

Alys passed out cups and poured tea.

"There's nothing like a common enemy to make people work together," said Soon.

Tets quipped, "I had a coach like that in school." That drew some chuckles.

As Alys handed a tea cup to Marcus her fingers caressed his.

"So what are we going to do?" asked Welly.

Marcus answered, "The plan is to do our trades and go straight home. Until the Captain says otherwise we're going to stay with that. When we get home, we can all tell people what we saw. Then the politicians argue about what to do."

"God help us all," said Betty.

***

Bridge Yaeger didn't like working at breakfast. It was the one meal where he could chat with his wife instead of talking business. But he'd been away for two months visiting the other six systems he governed from Corwynt. Now that he was back, all the decisions that couldn't be delegated were waiting for him.

So, breakfast was early, his wife was asleep, and bureaucrats made reports standing across the table. Yaeger didn't invite them to sit. If it was unimportant enough that they didn't want to stand, it could wait until next week.

". . . for an effective three percent of total tax revenue," concluded the Director of Commerce. "Closing this inheritance loophole is essential for meeting our Censorial obligations and should be done immediately."

The Director held out a tablet with the text of the revised tax law for the gubernatorial thumbprint.

Yaeger kept chewing his eggs. He could have swallowed them right off the fork, but he wanted to savor them. Today it was real bird eggs, flown down from the North Pole Archipelago. If the job made him deal with poltroons such as this one, he'd damn well enjoy the perks as well.

He swallowed and said, "No."

The Director inhaled to object, but shut up at Yeager's wave.

"This is Corwynt. Real estate and businesses don't belong to people, they belong to families. If we try to change that they'll go into hysterics. I'm not calling in the Dragoons so you can squeeze three percent out of these people. There're better places to push on the budget."

The governor let 'such as your staff' go unstated.

"What else?" Yeager took another delicious forkful of scrambled eggs.

The Director reeled off a list of statistics. All were in the normal range. Yeager asked for them to check for fluctuations the Director might not mention.

It ended with, "Merchant ships are in port from the planets Lompoc, Shian, . . ." The director listed a dozen more worlds. Only one was unfamiliar to the Governor.

"Fiera?" he asked.

A tap on the Director's tablet brought up more details. "The *Azure Tarn*, carrying refined metals from Fwynwr Ystaen. It's making an extended stay to establish relationships with local businesses. Most of the crew is unmarried."

Yeager laughed. "Ah, bringing bachelors to marry into a clan. Those people know how to do business on Corwynt. You could learn from them."

He didn't remember a Fiera. Which was odd. He knew all the

inhabited worlds in the provinces bordering his own. No point in asking the Director. He wasn't cleared for any information outside their own province.

The governor waved him aside for the next bureaucrat.

The Director of Order stepped forward, forcing Commerce to scoot aside to avoid an elbow.

"Good morning, Governor Yeager. There are eight death sentences awaiting your approval."

He put his fork down. Best not to eat during this part.

***

Landry knew an invitation to visit Goch Home "as soon as practical" was not good news. When the usual chat with a dozen relatives was reduced to a wave and "good evening" while they went straight to Vychan's study, it had to be bad news.

Then the broker unlocked the cabinet with the *good* brandy.

Landry sniffed the fumes as his hands warmed the glass. "How bad is it? The Censorate coming to kill us?"

Vychan poured himself a little bit, drank it, then filled it halfway. "Not yet. But I do owe you an apology."

This called for a sip of brandy. Best to let the native explain at his own pace.

"Secret societies are supposed to keep our existence, or at least our membership, secret. We want to share what we know. Carefully, so as not to bring the Censorate down on us. We'll send out a rogue net message or write something on a wall. If someone reacts we watch them to see if they're a Censorial infiltrator or a potential recruit. If they look good, we'll test them."

He sighed.

"We're supposed to protect our knowledge. Keeping it from being lost. Each member has their own cache. And sometimes societies will exchange secrets. There's a competition there. When members of two historical societies meet, they want to brag. 'My secrets are more precious than your secrets.' Or they run down a third group. 'That's not real history, it's an old novel.'"

"Which could have some good data in it," said Landry with a chuckle.

"Oh, yes. That's the whole problem with our situation. How can we *know*? Nyrath is reluctant to exchange. The Censorate has created false data in the past to subvert us. We haven't caught them doing it recently. They're getting lazy."

Landry tossed back some more brandy. "Good thing for us."

"Yes." Vychan tilted the bottle to refill his glass, realized he hadn't drunk any, and put it back down. He took a swig before talking again.

"Nyrath declared the existence of the history text secret. But. He's allowing us to share what year it is. And every member with connections to any other secret society promptly told them. To gloat."

That called for another sip. Landry asked, "Will the Censorate hear about it?"

"Probably already has. That is, some collaborator has told his handler. It will take a while to move up through the bureaucracy to someone with the courage to take action."

"What will they do?"

Vychan grimaced. He gulped some brandy with less respect than the vintage deserved. "Something. Most of the records we've tagged as Censorial forgeries are calendars or other time records. They make a big deal of their permanence. Million-year Censorate. If we can disprove that it cuts deep. So they'll act. I don't know what it'll be. Usual slow investigation, unless someone panics."

Landry stood and walked a few paces, as far as he could in the office. "I'm wondering if I should panic. Lift off and head for home." The storm damage was repaired and tanks topped off. They could fly out today.

"Not yet. Nyrath's kept them all from saying Fiera. They'll have to interrogate someone from my society to get your ship. And this is a very suspicious time for you to leave. We're in the middle of the trades. If you've offloaded some cargo and take off without receiving your payment, the Censorials will notice. You don't want to be noticed like that."

"No." Landry sat. "We'll sit tight then."

***

Welly made an impression on Dilwyn Goch at the dance. Or, he was helping out his sister Argel. Either way, going on a double date with Roger seemed a pleasant way to spend an evening.

Dilwyn's suggestion of a show followed by dinner brought them to a movie theater on the middle level. It felt like home. The holographic projector wasn't superior to Fieran technology. The seats were comfortable. The big difference was snacking on fried seaweed instead of popcorn.

"Four Sisters" was a romantic comedy, Corwynt style. A money-losing factory needed experts who could put it on the right track. The eligible daughters of the clan needed to find them, woo them, and marry them, while resisting the temptation to marry out of the clan.

A series of implausible meet-cutes found a salesman, engineer, and efficiency expert. Personality clashes were solved by pairing them with a different sister from the one who'd met them. The fourth sister was freed to marry out to her true love, not to be seen again in the movie.

The climax was seeing the factory's new products roll off the production line as the sisters packed them into boxes. Welly looked left and right to check Dilwyn and Argel's faces. They thought it was a happy ending. A single tear ran down Argel's cheek.

Leaving single-file with the crowd kept them from chatting. The first chance to talk was on the escalator up to the next level. Welly drank in the sights of the city's interior. This was her first time here at night. No stars were visible through the clear walls. Instead, they reflected the lights of the interior. Most were fixed and a boring white, but there were enough colored, blinking, and moving to make it more beautiful than any night sky she'd seen on Fiera.

"Careful." Dilwyn grabbed her arm as Welly reached the end of the escalator.

She stumbled, leaned on him to recover, and thanked him. "Sorry. I should watch my feet."

"There's no shame in that. It is an impressive sight, isn't it? I'm too used to it to really appreciate it."

Dilwyn led them around the corner of the ardal. On the structure's wall the words "The Grey Feather" were scrawled across a thirty foot painting of a bird's feather.

His sister stopped. "Dilwyn! What account are you charging this to?"

"Half our personal allowances, half to Marketing."

"Marketing! You can't—"

"Argel, they're *clients*."

"Still, you—"

"And I talked to Uncle Vychan and received permission."

"Oh." Argel took Roger's arm and started walking again.

Welly understood the objections once they entered the restaurant. There were no spacers among the people waiting for a table. Just well-dressed locals and Censorials with lots of braid on their uniforms.

The walls were top to bottom photographs of sea birds in flight, or diving through the shadows of a kelp jungle. One showed a nest woven of kelp leaves floating on the water, full of eggs.

The hostess' doubt faded away as Dilwyn proved they were on time for his reservation. The foursome was seated in a high-backed booth. Leather-upholstered walls gave them privacy from the next table.

"Whoa, this place doesn't serve any fish?" asked Welly as she scrolled through the dishes displayed on the tabletop.

"They have a few. Hidden at the end of the list. For people who don't like trying new things." Dilwyn flipped back and forth among a few options.

Welly could tell the whole roasted kelpgull was tempting him. She checked the price. No wonder he was undecided. That had to be steep even for the clan marketing budget.

"Ooh, pot pie." Roger stabbed his choice.

Argel leaned over to look. "A what?"

"That's what we call meat in pastry back home," he explained.

Welly settled for a breast with some local spices she'd liked on fish. Once everyone made their choices the table blanked. A waiter delivered drinks.

"How did you like the movie?" asked Dilwyn.

"It was fascinating," said Welly. "Everything's so different from back home. My parents wouldn't care what my future husband did for a living as long as he could support me and our children. My brothers and I moved out as soon as we were old enough to be on our own."

"Like other worlds," sighed Argel. "Everyone free."

Dilwyn countered, "Sounds lonely. And you, Roger? What did you think of the show?"

The other spacer took a sip of his wine. "I agree, it gave me a lot of insight into your culture. I was surprised by how rough a production it was. My high school drama club insisted on better acting."

Welly frowned at him. She didn't want to criticize their hosts.

Argel looked puzzled. "Acting?"

"Um." Roger thought of examples. "Okay. When her husband told the oldest sister, he'd landed a contract for a thousand of the new widgets, she was happy. The actress looked really happy.

"Compare that to the scene where the youngest married the guy she'd been mooning after the whole movie. She was happy to finally be with him. She was also sad to be leaving her family. But she didn't look happy and sad. The actress just calmly said these words about how happy and sad she was."

"It's fiction," said Argel. "You have to fill in stuff like that."

"But I didn't have to fill it in for the oldest sister. She could act."

"That's why Fflur Danna had the lead part. She's talented," said Dilwyn.

"But out of a whole planet why is there only one talented actress?"

Argel shook her head. "The whole planet isn't making the movie. Just the Danna clan. Less than two hundred people. I think they're 'acting' better than our clan would."

That brought a laugh from Welly. "Oh, God. That clan must have lots of wanna-be actors trying to marry in."

"They do," answered Argel. "If you look at the gossip sites they're all about what some Danna guy did to a girl who wanted to be in a movie. But they need writers, camera operators, editors, lots of people.

Not just actors."

Dilwyn said, "I think that explains my problem with the writing."

Then the food arrived and there was no time for movies.

Welly liked the poultry. It didn't taste like chicken. Maybe like a chicken whose diet was entirely fish.

Desert was an amazing egg and sugar thing Dilwyn urged on them all. Afterwards a stroll to let dinner settle seemed like a good idea. The Goch family warehouses weren't what Welly would pick for sightseeing, but it seemed normal to the locals.

The couples split up to tour the facilities. Dilwyn pointed out the cargo handling gear, with an amusing anecdote of how he'd nearly caused a forklift accident as a teen. "Of course the real heart of the business is knowing all the manufacturers in the city, and in as many other cities as we can. We get to know spacers, too. Then we introduce those that have and those that need, and there's a deal."

Welly realized what was happening. *Crap. He's not boasting to impress me so he can get into my pants. This is courting here. He's showing how profitable the business is so I'll marry in.*

"Are you going to be a broker, then? Or running the warehouse?"

"Broker, if I can prove I'm good at it. I've been doing the legwork for some of Uncle Vychan's deals."

Welly made an impressed sound.

"So . . . you don't talk much about what you do on the ship."

She perched on a crate, bringing her eye level up to his. "Not much to say. I'll allocate power or handle communications. I've even sat as pilot if there's nothing around to run into."

"You don't like the life?"

"I like the ship. The crew are good people. Mostly. But I'm not going to make a life of it. I just wanted some adventure before settling down." Welly laughed. "I sure found that on this trip."

Dilwyn leaned in. "Would staying here be settling down, or an adventure?"

She didn't know how to answer that. His kiss said she didn't need to.

***

They parted from their dates at the tram station. Once they were out of sight of the platform, Welly said, "I think Dilwyn is serious about me."

"They're serious people," answered Roger.

She looked at him. "Does Argel want you to stay?"

He tugged his collar closed. "No. She wants out of this town."

***

The Governor escorted his wife into the Censorial Residence's grand dining hall. Instead of the normal banquet table it held only a small circular one set for two.

She clutched his arm. "Bridge! Where is everyone?"

He kissed her cheek. "I don't know. I told them to go away and didn't ask. Happy anniversary, Dulcinea."

"Darling! You remembered!"

"Of course I didn't. Petra told me. She had a list of presents picked out for me to choose from. Fancy ways to show I have more money than time."

Dulcinea laughed. "I was expecting a ruby necklace."

"That was on the list. But then I'd spend tonight seeing you wear it while I talked to people I didn't want to talk to."

Yeager pulled out her chair and slid it in under her. As he took his own seat the servants moved in. Singh, the Residence's head butler, poured the wine himself. The soup, salad, and fish courses were all set out together.

Then Singh followed the rest of the servants out, closing the grand doors of the hall behind him.

"Good heavens," said Dulcinea. "I can't remember when we were last this alone."

Yeager smiled. "Singh will be back to check on us."

She sampled the soup, then scooped up a full spoonful and savored it. Rather than take another she put the spoon down. "Bridge, can you afford to do this? You're offending some powerful people."

"Not the most powerful. Tonight's dinner was all second tier. Or worse. It would have been arguing procurement and appointments. Those can all wait."

"Then tell me about your trip. What was the worst part?"

He chuckled. "Vulkoro, the planetary proconsul for Lompoc. Spent the entire time trying to convince me to hire him on as a provincial director."

"Which department?" she asked.

"He didn't care as long as it was a stepping stone back to the Censorial capital."

"Ah."

"I'm tempted to leave him on Lompoc until he dies, but that's not a nice thing to do to the other seventy-some million people on the planet."

Dulcinea diverted him to other parts of the trip, extracting humorous anecdotes and trading tales from old trips of hers. They laughed and talked, only interrupting to say 'thank you' as new courses were placed.

"—and by then we were so desperate for some fresh air, we were glad to stop at Sierra—"

"Fiera?" he blurted.

"No, Sierra Padre. Only half terraformed, air so thin you can't run, and hardly a single flat spot on the whole planet. They advertise a ski resort, but I didn't try it. Why? What's Fiera?"

"A ship came in from there, and I can't remember where it is." Yaeger thanked Singh as delicate cups of sorbet were placed in front of them.

"It's a big Censorate."

"I know. But I need to know what's going on in my corner of it. If a ship came here from another province I want to know why. Did they take a wrong turn in hyper? Are the currents shifting to bring it closer? Or is it a stalking horse for some governor who wants to strengthen his province at the expense of mine?"

"Most likely simple traders, I'd expect."

"Most likely. But in a big Censorate the *unlikely* will always be happening somewhere."

"Look it up then. *You* can."

Yeager smiled. "I'm tempted. But I'm too busy to take time out to go to the vault for curiosity."

"And for my curiosity? I've never seen your sanctum."

He scraped the last of the melted sorbet from the cup. "I'd thought of taking you dancing, or to a show. Not to the basement of the city."

"I won't get a good night's sleep if you're fretting about this."

An hour later four grim members of the governor's guards rode with them in a hovercar to the bottom infrastructure levels of Arnvon City. The entrance to the vault was manned by ten Censorial Dragoons. Not that an attack in force was considered a danger. The number was to prevent bribe attempts.

Once past the Dragoons, Yeager supplied the vault door with some blood for DNA checking, and a look at his retina and fingerprints. That earned him the right to supply the code word for entry. He was careful not to use the alternate word which indicated he was under duress.

Then it was just Bridge and Dulcinea Yeager sealed into a six meter square room. The vault slammed shut, forcing in enough air to make her ears pop.

"*Now* we're alone," he said.

Dulcinea surveyed it. Overflowing bookshelves. Stellar maps of normal and hyperspace. Military-looking electronic boxes of every shape and size piled on the floor. A small table with a folding chair held a computer, seemingly no different from the one in Bridge's office. A standard battery pack lay next to it.

Bridge was already examining the star maps in search of his mystery planet. She drifted along the bookshelves, reading titles but not picking up any books. No sense testing her husband's tolerance by pushing on the 'need to know' rule.

Besides, 'CONTINGENCY PLAN FOR GENERAL WORK STOPPAGE' and 'NAVAL COUNTER-INFILTRATION TEST PROCEDURES' didn't seem like page turners.

He pulled a book off a shelf, muttering, "I don't see it on the maps. Maybe it's an outpost." After skimming the table of contents, he exchanged the book for another.

The labels on the military gear meant nothing to Dulcinea. She suspected Bridge didn't understand them either. It was the kind of stuff kept secure by training people in a whole new language for using it.

"Damnit," said the governor. "It's not in any of the neighboring provinces. Or the ones neighboring them. Which is all I have."

"Time to turn that on?" she asked, pointing at the computer.

"No. Every time it's turned on it sends a notification to the local Navy squadron commander and the Censorial capital. I don't want to attract attention."

"You could simply go to the ship and ask them."

"Let a thousand bureaucrats know that's a worry point for me? They'd love to have something like that to leverage me with."

She watched him wrestle with it.

At last he let out a sigh. "I bet I'm worried over nothing. Some damn clerk wrote down the name of their home city as the planet. I'll make them recheck it."

"Let's turn in then."

***

The hangar door stayed open in good weather. Corwynt apparently only had good weather and hurricanes. Roger and Soon sat at the picnic table, leisurely lunching on sandwiches.

One of the two-seater floatcars pulled up before the hangar. The smartly uniformed young Censorial officer who'd welcomed them to Corwynt emerged.

"Crap," muttered Roger. He realized he should have brought a comm unit so he could warn the ship of an inspection. He raised his voice. "Good afternoon, sir!"

The Censorial walked over to them. The Fierans stood.

"I am Ensign Koing. I'm looking for the crew of the *Azure Tarn*."

Roger replied, "We're both on the crew, sir."

"I need to confirm some information. What is the ship's home system?"

"Fiera."

The officer scribbled on his tablet. "Planet?"

"Fiera. It's the first planet settled in the system."

"Spelled the same way?"

"Yes, sir. F – I – E – R – A."

More scribbling. "And city?"

Roger didn't have an answer to that. Soon jumped in. "We're registered out of Argos Station, the high port."

"Thank you for your cooperation."

The Censorial walked back to his floater. His native driver sped off as soon as he was seated.

"What was that about?" wondered Roger.

Soon said, "I don't know, but we'd better tell the captain."

***

"A really great deal on used floaters" were words to make Captain Landry wary. Marcus was busy at the Goch warehouse again so he took both Gander and Tets along to inspect them. Fieran engineers could reverse engineer used equipment as well as new . . . but only if it worked in the first place.

As the trio ascended the escalator toward the dealer's shop Landry noticed a cleaning bot hovering by the underside of the structure. It was erasing some graffiti.

"Crap." The escalator didn't stop, but Landry's body stiffened as he unconsciously tried to resist going closer.

Gander looked around for a threat. "Trouble, sir?"

"Not—immediately."

The graffiti was the number 3756—the current year in the Gregorian calendar. It must have been written by one of the members of Vychan's secret society, or someone they'd told, or . . . how far had that little fact spread?

"Something wrong with that number?" asked Gander.

Landry realized he'd been staring. He turned to face the other side. "It's . . . well, call it a political statement against the Censorate."

"Good," snapped Tets. "It sucks."

"It does," agreed Gander. "But I don't want to be in the crossfire when they start shooting rebels."

"Rebels should shoot them. Maybe we sell them some guns next trip." Tets mimed holding a rifle.

"Shut up, for God's sake," said Landry. "There could be a microphone in the railing."

The silence continued until they reached Ilar's Reliable Vehicles.

***

A card game was running in *Azure Tarn's* galley when Welly came home. The players glanced at the chronometer. Almost an hour past midnight. She drew a tall glass of water from the sink, gulped it down, and refilled it.

"Thirsty work?" asked Soon.

"Uh-huh. Dance class. Dilwyn was spinning me around the ballroom all evening." Welly sipped more water.

Betty stage-whispered, "Not a mattress?"

Soon kicked her in the ankle.

"I liked the dance they invited us all to." Roger tossed the king of hearts into the middle then collected all four cards.

"Those were all easy," said Welly. "There were some really fun ones tonight."

He gave her a look. "I think I'll stick to the easy ones."

Soon led with the deuce of trumps. "Is Dilwyn a good teacher?"

"Hell, no. He'd never done some of them before. I think I was learning faster than him." Welly smirked. "Or it's easier when I'm not leading."

Roger sacrificed a club and shoved the trick toward Betty. "So where is this leading? He sounds serious."

The glass tilted up as Welly finished it. "Yeah. Too serious maybe. He'd be good for a fling. But he wants something steady."

"Looking to breed you?" asked Betty.

"Maybe. More that he needs to be married if he wants a promotion. They won't give real responsibility to somebody who might marry out."

Soon looked up from her cards. "It's for a raise? That'd kill a relationship for me."

"No, it's not like that. More that you're not really an adult until you're married and have kids of your own."

"Run away, girl." Betty played the ten of spades.

"I don't know. He's tempting me."

That stopped the card game. Even Alys, who'd been ignoring the conversation, put down her cards.

"Seriously? You'd jump ship?" demanded Soon.

"The Articles allow us to resign at any port."

Roger said, "It's not the ship. It's your family, Fiera, everything you're leaving behind."

That made Welly twist her mouth in a bitter smirk. "My family's no loss. There's a reason I became a spacer."

"You want to live under the fucking Censorate?" said Betty.

Welly shrugged. "I don't like the Censorate. But a lot of places suck back home. People are *happy* here."

Alys said, "Lots are happy back home."

"Lots aren't. Nobody dies alone here. You're part of a big family."

"Strange attitude for somebody who wanted to get away from her family," countered Betty.

"It's—it's different." Welly waved her hands as she tried to verbalize her idea.

The rest waited quietly.

"Okay. If you have a little family, mom, dad, two kids, and one goes bad, there's nobody in the family to fight back. Back home there's spouses beaten, kids beaten, and nobody knows until they wind up in the hospital."

Tears shone in Welly's eyes. She took a couple of deep breaths.

"Here's it's a big family. At least a hundred people. If anyone gets nasty there's cousins, uncles, grandmothers around. They keep assholes in check. You can find someone you like in the family. You're safe."

Soon said, "That makes sense . . . but I'd think it could still go bad. A small clique of assholes on top can make everyone else miserable. I was in a company like that. Got out as fast as I could."

"That's what happens here. Dilwyn told me a story of a clan that went bad like that." She topped off her glass and sat at the end of the table.

"The oldest generation all died or went senile. Four couples took charge of the clan. They had the key positions in the clan business and intimidated the others in their generation. Started throwing their weight around. Spending clan money on luxuries for themselves, not doing their share of scut work, pushing people just to make them submit."

The deck of cards had been reshuffled for the next deal. Welly picked it up.

"The young people didn't invite anyone to marry in. They took any chance to marry out." Welly took a dozen cards off the deck and dropped them on the table.

"That meant fewer people to do the scut work and more pressure from the clique on top. The middle-aged folk who'd married in divorced and went back to their birth clans." Another dozen cards landed on the table.

"Then those divorcees married out to rejoin their exes." A dozen more.

"By now there's a lot less people to boss around and still the same amount of work for the clan business. But the clan has such a bad reputation no one wants to marry them. So the ones who wanted to marry out join the Censorial Service. Or run away to the Jaaphisii. Even suicide." With each phrase a few more cards were discarded.

"Nothing left but the clique on top." Welly fanned out the cards left in her hand. "Couldn't run the factory. Defaulted on their contracts. Used up their credit."

"Did they starve?" asked Roger.

"Maybe they would have," said Welly. "But a clan with more people than work bought the factory and the clanhold to split off a daughter clan. All the price the clique could ask was room and board until they died. They lived their last days on mediocre food served by people who mocked them. And clan Thwylla is still a word to stop someone abusing his authority."

Betty gathered up the cards and began to shuffle.

Alys said, "If it happened once, it can happen again. We won't be here for you to go home to if the Goch clan goes bad."

"I know," said Welly. "But there's people marrying into Clan Goch. So they think it's going to stay healthy."

Cards skimmed across the table as Betty dealt out the deck. "How about we play and Welly screws up her life on her own?"

***

Vychan was already seated when Landry entered the spaceport tavern. The broker waved, almost bouncing in his seat.

"The deals are set," he said as Landry joined him at the table. "Everyone's agreed. We can start the transfers."

"Good. How long is this going to take?"

"About four or five days for all the swaps." Vychan unrolled a display on the table, shoving a bowl of chips aside to make room. "Here's the sequence."

The diagram was a flowchart, a dozen nodes each marked with the logo of a clan business. The arrows wore illustrations of the goods being traded and notes with quantities and other information. The flow split and rejoined in the middle for a few nodes for extra complexity.

The Fieran shook his head. "I don't think I could handle doing business here."

"Oh, it's usually not this bad. For a while I was afraid we'd have to use cash to patch over some of the links, and bring the Censorial tax collectors in on it all. But this way it's all exchanging goods of roughly equal value, which the Censorials ignore."

"I appreciate that."

"I as well. Now we celebrate."

The barmaid arrived with plates of what seemed to be spaghetti noodles in green sauce. "Special today," she declared.

The 'noodles' turned out to be shellfish tentacles. Tasty ones, to

Landry's relief. Corwynti cuisine didn't always agree with him but this was delicious.

"Nautili are scarce," said Vychan, "but the cook here has shoaler cousins who gave him first option on a catch. Pricey, but today is a day to indulge."

After a few more bites the broker said, "We should have a more thorough celebration after your cargo is loaded. May we have a dance in your honor at Goch Home?"

"Of course. We'd enjoy that very much." Landry thought a few of his crew would be downright thrilled.

"Splendid. I'll have the trucks at your ship this afternoon. We'll have the rest of your cargo offloaded and start the trades tomorrow. You'll be on your way home in less than a week."

"Good." Landry traced the exchanges on the display, now obscured in a few spots by dots of sauce. "What is your profit in this venture?"

"Oh, we take a percentage here and there. I'll have a crate of your toys, some machine tools, and furniture. The last we'll take home instead of keeping in the warehouse for future deals. There's beds grown too creaky for comfort. Time we replaced them."

***

Governor Yaeger wasn't pleased by confirmation the ship came from "Fiera." The vault computer held a database of every planet in the Censorate. But on his appointment as governor, the District Monitor made it clear that was for emergencies only. Mere curiosity was no excuse for accessing restricted information.

No matter how curious he became about that damn ship. He wished it'd landed here at Arnvon. A casual tour would let him 'accidentally' run into it. But Bundoran was a third of the way around the planet. No visit there would be casual.

He tried to put it out of his mind. If his subordinates noticed he was distracted, they'd maneuver to cut into their rivals' budgets, or try to trick him into letting restricted information slip.

Then the idea hit him. If the Fieran ship traversed three or more provinces to reach Corwynt, it was unparalleled among merchant vessels. It was almost more probable that a shift in hyperspace changed the travel distance between two points in normal space.

Such shifts were to be reported at once. The penalties for failing to do so were harsh. The ship would be confiscated. The captain and navigator would be rigorously interrogated to discover the new path. If they'd used it for political ends, executions would follow.

The carrot side of dealing with hyperspace shifts was a substantial reward, intended to exceed the profit in evading Censorial tariffs for several voyages.

If this ship found such a route and landed here, on one of the least loyal planets on this side of the Censorial capital . . . why?

The paranoid answer was, 'Because they came from another disloyal planet and were trying to synchronize a revolt.'

A certain measure of paranoia was required in Yeager's position. Too much became a self-fulfilling prophecy. His predecessors were more likely to be relieved by Censorial decree than assassinated by the locals . . . but Corwynt was fonder of assassination than any nearby world.

That aspect meant he couldn't frighten Dulcinea by talking to her about it. So he brooded.

If there was a chance of a multi-planet conspiracy, Yeager needed to take action. But not any action that would make him look foolish to the Censorial Court. There were always new favorites ready to replace a governor who no longer held the Censor's confidence.

So he waited a week before visiting the vault again.

If Fiera was a loyal planet only a couple provinces away, there was no need to worry. If it was a nest of rebels on the far side of the galaxy, he'd have justification for a treason trial. Yeager wasn't sure which result he preferred, just that he wanted either over some mushy answer that left him undecided.

Turning on the computer didn't improve his mood. The battery slot was blocked by a mechanical lock. Yeager hadn't used it during his term in office, and by the feel as he wrestled with it, his predecessor may have never opened the lock. Finally, the tumblers gave way. He jammed the battery in.

A few moments left him wondering if he'd face the lesser embarrassment of asking the Dragoon guards outside for a fresh battery.

Then the screen lit up. The routine announcements that the computer woke up scrolled by. Then: 'NOTIFICATION SENT: CENSORIAL SECURITY MINISTRY. NOTIFICATION SENT: DISTRICT MONITOR. NOTIFICATION SENT: CENSORIAL NAVY SQUADRON CORWYNT.'

"Nice to have that over with," muttered Yeager. Then he sat down and began typing.

Censorial Security preferred the crudest interface for restricted data. Graphics, decision support, and context sensing were all ways an enemy could infiltrate. A screen of monochrome text lit the governor's face.

The astrographic database was easy to access. It even included some data from the Censorial Census. Searches could be made by star, planet, city, or geographic feature.

It promptly informed Yeager there was no planet 'Fiera' in the Censorate. Nor was there a 'Feira', 'Fierah', 'Feera', or 'Phiera'. Some persuasion disgorged a list of planets beginning with 'F'. None approximated the one he was looking for.

Yeager formulated a new, very simple hypothesis. He shot to his feet, knocking the chair into a stack of encryption gear. "They lied to me. Those miserable greedy merchants lied to me!"

He controlled his anger. After a few deep breaths he shut down the computer. With a sigh he pulled out the battery and twisted the lock closed again.

Thinking about the amount of time he'd wasted on this lie infuriated him. It wasn't a lie to him. It was a lie to the Censor.

At least he'd be able to execute them all for wasting his time.

The Dragoons and Guards came to attention as he opened the vault door. It sounded like he'd interrupted another story of how much harder Dragoon training was in the good old days before the

Governor's Guards retired from the Censorial Dragoons for easier duty.

Yeager snapped, "Lieutenant. Secure line."

"Yessir," said the officer. He produced a thick box from a labeled cabinet.

It was answered by the secure relay operator, who only nodded when told "Director of Order."

A minute went by before the screen lit up. "Governor Yeager. How may I serve you?" In the background was a dinner table with half full plates, and the director's wife ushering children out of the room.

"The ship *Azure Tarn* is at Bundoran Spaceport. It is the Will of the Censor that the ship be impounded and the crew independently interrogated."

Director Yokat swallowed. A Governor had the right to speak with Censorial authority . . . but Yeager had never wielded it before. "Yes sir. Interrogated for what?"

"For their biographies, Director."

"At once, sir."

***

Police Liaison Glain frowned warily at her opponent's queen, sitting in the middle of the chessboard. Subcommandant Jamal didn't make such mistakes. It had to be a trap.

Behind her one of the enlisted men answered the comm. "Censorial Investigative Service Planetary Operations Center, Investigator Second Class Li speaking, how may I help you?"

Glain thought the boy sounded quite alert for the night shift. He must have been indulging in the imported coffee. She didn't dare. Once she went back to regular police work she'd never be able to afford it. No sense picking up an addiction she'd have to break.

Everyone jumped as Li's cup sprang into the air, splashing coffee over a holoprojector. Li stood at attention. "Yes, sir. At once, sir."

The Chief Investigator stepped toward the comm console. Li ignored him, waving frantically at Jamal.

"What?" demanded the officer.

"It's Director Yokat," hissed Li.

Another cup fell. The table shook as Jamal shoved it aside to reach the comm. Not, alas, hard enough to knock the chess pieces over.

"Sir, I am Subcommandant Jamal, the watch officer."

Glain followed Jamal to listen in on the conversation. It was, after all, her duty to know what the CIS was doing so she could arrange the support of local law enforcement.

Then she heard the phrase "Will of the Censor." No, locals would not be welcome on this assignment. Glain stayed silent as Jamal finished the call with more "sirs."

Jamal pulled up Bundoran on the map board. "Falling rocks, that's in Regional Commandant Feliz's jurisdiction." He hesitated.

Even Glain knew the commandant's reputation for savaging subordinates who woke her. She was unsurprised when Jamal typed out the arrest order for *Azure Tarn's* crew.

"Should that be 'Eyes only'?" she suggested.

"Hmmm. Safer that way." Jamal added the restriction to the message and sent it to the regional headquarters in Caernod.

'Eyes only' would keep any eager subordinate from bringing the message to Feliz's quarters. The commandant wouldn't see it until she arrived at her desk, an hour or three after waking.

While Jamal logged the event in the POC diary, Glain returned to the chessboard. Now she saw the trap. If her bishop took Jamal's queen, the open file would let his rook through for a checkmate.

When he reseated himself she moved a knight to threaten the queen. The rest of the game was only interrupted by an hourly status check. When Jamal offered a rook as bait for her bishop Glain took it and acted surprised by the mate.

"That was a tough match," said Jamal. "May I make it up to you with lunch at Llion's?"

That would be social, not professional, if Jamal had his way. Glain had been mildly encouraging the flirtation to keep the Censorial happy. But tonight she had a higher priority.

"I'd love to, but I promised Grandmother I'd take my lunch break with the clan if I could. But . . ." Glain pretended a thought had struck her. "I think she'd like to meet you. May I ask her permission to invite you to dinner at our home?"

His face lit up. "Why, yes!"

She locked the giggles inside until she was on the escalator down. Censorials were all assigned to planets far from their homeworld. Meeting parents was a major relationship milestone, often happening after the wedding. On Corwynt a young man often was forced to meet the parents, grandparents, and uncles before he could speak to the girl who'd intrigued him.

Once done laughing she used her handcomm to call home. Cousin Aderyn answered the kitchen line. "Yes, dear?"

"I'm on my break. Anything warm on the stove?" That was a code phrase in case there were any Censorial eavesdroppers.

"A pot of chowder. The shellfish were on the shoals only ten hours ago."

"Sounds delicious. I'll see you in five minutes."

Aderyn would be sure to tell anyone asking that Glain had come home for a meal. And likely send a few youngsters on errands to confuse anyone watching the door.

Glain took a cross-belt to the other side of the arcology, visiting an ardal she'd never seen before. The Iwan clanhome didn't have anyone on night watch. The sleepy youngster who finally answered the buzzer was impressed enough by her police uniform to bring her right in.

Glain bullied him into taking her directly to Cadfan's bedroom. The boy had enough spine to make her wait in the hall while he woke his elder.

Cadfan Iwan emerged in a gray bathrobe. He stared at Glain for a moment before telling the boy, "Thank you, lad. Back to bed now."

As the youngster padded off Cadfan led her to a nook with three soft chairs. He fell into one, yawned, and said, "Didn't I do the security lecture a month or two ago? Do I have to do it at every meeting? You should not be here. It's a risk. You could get us all arrested."

"It's important. A Will of the Censor arrest order is out for a ship from a planet I've never heard of. It's on Bundoran. I'm thinking it might be who we heard 3756 from." Glain shared the exact words of the order.

That woke Cadfan up. He leaned back as he thought through the logic. The first new history they'd learned in decades. An arrest order for treason or something equally important. Nobody had stabbed a bureaucrat lately. The arrest was probably for the historians.

"What do you want me to do?"

"You heard the year from somebody. Pass the arrest news back so it gets to the source."

"Um." Cadfan rubbed his stubbled chin. "How long do we have?"

"Right now the order is in an inbox waiting for office hours to start in Caernod. Then relayed to Bundoran and a team deployed. Six hours. Maybe twelve."

"Drown it. I can't go in person. Too out of pattern. I'll call him."

"You sure? They could listen in."

Cadfan grinned. "That, my dear, is why we have code words. Now go. Can you find your way out?"

Glain nodded and left.

The head of their secret society went down the hall to his office. He ran the necessary code words through his mind. He needed to make sense to any eavesdropping Censorial analyst.

His contact was the head of a rival history preservation group. Sometimes Cadfan wondered if the entire native population of Corwynt was involved in secret societies of one type or another.

It took a minute for the comm screen to light up. Then Cadfan regretted not making the call audio only. Emyr Tolog bore a terrifying amount of chest hair.

"You interrupted a lovely dream. Justify yourself," growled Emyr.

"I just woke from a dream too. You were having a dish of poached sea urchin at a café in Bundoran. They were serving three thousand seven hundred and fifty-six plates. With carbonated chocolate milk for dessert."

Cadfan paused to watch the other take it in. He seemed to be decoding it properly.

"But first you made your reservations at an office in Caernod. You must call before office hours start and all the reservations are full."

Emyr nodded firmly. "That's a fascinating dream, but couldn't you tell it to me in the morning?"

A wave of relief went through Cadfan as he heard the acknowledgement code word, but he didn't let it reach his face. "I was afraid I'd forget the important parts."

"Go back to bed."

***

Azure Tarn moved out of the hanger to one of the open landing pads for loading cargo. They'd be gone before the next storm. Captain Landry didn't want to pay for another month of hangar rent.

The crates of spare parts were easy to load. They could stack on top of each other or be hooked to the tie-down points scattered on the deck and bulkheads of the cargo hold. It was the vehicles that were giving Marcus Landry fits. He'd sent members of the Goch clan back to pick up more tie-down straps twice and they were getting close to running out again.

Captain Landry watched his son work with a calm expression. The point of making Marcus the supercargo was to train him in how to make decisions on his own. He was certainly learning that today. Besides, the captain didn't have any better ideas on how to arrange things. A mix of floaters, air cars, and other antigrav transports would not stack in any convenient fashion.

The captain's mind drifted off to calculations of how much they could make selling this once they returned home to Fiera. At the very least he'd be able to pay off the note on his ship and invest in some upgrades. Or, not that he seriously considered it, sell the ship and enjoy a wealthy retirement. If he managed to get a bidding war among outfits wanting to reverse engineer the floaters to discover how the Censorate had such efficient antigrav . . . well, he could pay for some serious castles in the air with that kind of money.

The fantasy math was interrupted by the approach of a one-man scooter, floating across the concrete of the spaceport. The driver would be collecting some fines if spaceport security saw how he was cutting corners on the painted lanes, as well as violating the speed limits. It skidded to a stop between a couple of flat-top cargo loaders waiting their turn to go onboard.

The driver hopped off and trotted toward Vychan Goch as he oversaw the loading crew. Captain Landry walked over, wondering what the fuss was about.

"What the leaking hell are you doing here?" snarled Vychan.

"It's an emergency," said the stranger.

"No emergency justifies approaching me in public."

Then the captain realized where he'd heard the stranger's voice before. This was Nyrath, the leader of Vychan's secret society, preserving history banned by the Censorate on pain of death. No, they shouldn't be meeting in public, and he didn't want his ship and crew getting caught up in treasonable activity.

"There's an arrest order for your friends here."

"What? Why?"

"Don't know. Just that they're to be taken in for interrogation." Nyrath didn't even try to keep his voice down. Well, everyone in earshot was in the crew or one of Vychan's relatives, but still.

"How do you know?" demanded Captain Landry.

"We have friends everywhere. They passed us the word. The order is still coming through channels."

Vychan spat onto the concrete. "Even slow as the Censorials are, we don't have much time. We need to get you out of here."

"Yes, but . . ." Most of the vehicles they'd traded their exotic Fieran goods for were still sitting on the concrete. What was on board . . . well, it would turn a profit, but not enough to justify the risks they'd taken on this voyage.

But he couldn't sell any of it from a Censorial jail cell.

Landry pressed his hands to his temples trying to think.

"Where'd you get the word from?" asked Vychan.

"Dammit, I promised to keep it secret."

"Someone here or at regional headquarters?"

The stranger grudgingly said, "A friend in Caernod."

"Right, then." Vychan thought. "So Regional passes it to their Liaison, who calls the Order Sub-Director for Bundoran, who has to delegate to an actual arrest team . . . that'll be hours."

Captain Landry lowered his hands. "Any chance it'll be less than two hours?"

"I'd be shocked."

Nyrath nodded in agreement.

"Okay." Landry turned to Nyrath. "Thank you. We'll take it from here. Best be gone, and try not to be noticed as you go."

"I will. And—thank you for everything you did for us." He hurried back to his scooter.

The captain turned toward the open cargo hatch. "Supercargo!"

Marcus looked up in surprise. He wasn't used to being micromanaged. "Sir?"

"Belay securing cargo. Toss it aboard as fast as you can. We lift in two hours. We'll secure it in flight. Anything you can't fit by lift time we're abandoning."

Which was, of course, the sort of order his son's academy classes said should be met with a resignation lest the ship be endangered. Marcus's face clearly showed he was thinking of it. Then he looked at the retreating scooter and back to the captain. "Aye-aye."

Marcus stepped over to the PA. Through the hatch Landry could hear a muffled announcement directing all hands to join in cargo shifting.

"What can I do?" asked Vychan. "More people? I can get the warehouse crew."

"No, we have about as many hands as can fit now. Buy the chandlery out of tie-downs, vacctape, and, hell, plain rope. We'll just have to hope we can secure it all before we have to do any serious maneuvering. You can keep all the leftover floaters to pay for it."

"Don't worry about it," replied the native. He lowered his voice. "That book earned all the gear you need."

Captain Landry grunted. The history book they'd given away was probably the reason the Censorate wanted to strap his whole crew to an interrogation table.

***

Marcus stood on the deactivated floater, his weight on his left foot.
If he shifted to the right the floater would fall off the upside-down
liftvan it rested on. One hand held the end of a tie-down strap while
the other waved to the crane operator. "Closer, closer, port, port,
forward, hold and lower!"

The open-sided car landed on the floater, almost arm's reach from
him. A PSI instructor would decertify him for handling cargo so
recklessly. Marcus looped the tie-down through the car's uprights. He
hooked it on to the stack adjacent and activated the tightening spool.
In a minute car and floater were held snugly to the deck and other
cargo. Not what his supercargo training would consider secure, but it
would hold until they were off this world.

"Release it!" he called. The crane unhooked and slid away to pick
up the next used vehicle. Marcus picked his way down the stack. The
solid deck felt comforting after swaying cargo under his feet.

"Marcus, may I have a moment, please?" asked Wynny.

"Yes, but we're in a hurry. Trouble with the next set?" Marcus had
set her to lining up the functional vehicles ready to be loaded in.

"No, it's . . . um. I wanted to talk to you at the dance tonight."

"Yes, that's a shame. I was looking forward to the dance too." But
a Censorial prison would take the fun out of dancing.

She looked down at her feet—thinking of dancing maybe—then up
at him. "Marcus, have you thought of staying on Corwynt?"

"Well, no. I like it here. I want to learn more about it, yes, but I
can't now with whatever that Censorial mess is. And I'm needed on
board. We're going to be cleaning this mess up all the way back to
Fiera." He waved at the haphazardly stacked cargo beside them.

"Then—if there's that much work—do you need another spacer?
I've worked shifting cargo in the warehouse, and I've been up to orbit
twice, I don't get sick in free fall."

Marcus stammered, "We can't—there isn't an opening—Wynny,
we could be arrested or blown up today. We can't take someone on

board under those conditions. What the heck are you thinking?"

The native girl stepped forward, her shoe next to his, and lifted her head to press her lips against his. Not a quick peck, a firm kiss, long enough to be clear that it wasn't an accident or a formality. Then she stepped back, her face the frightened mask of someone who'd broken a rule and feared punishment.

Marcus was too surprised to breathe. The realization that thoughts and dreams he'd had were real, were shared, could become something greater froze him. He didn't know what to do and was terrified of ruining this perfect moment.

Then Wynny took another step back and started to turn. Marcus lunged forward, wrapped his arms around her, and pulled her into a kiss of his own. Her lips parted under the pressure of his. She pressed her body against him and slid her hands up his back.

They might have stayed that way forever if not for the noise of a floater crashing to the deck as it was deactivated for transport. They broke the kiss but Marcus kept hold of Wynny.

"I can't stay today," he said. "And you can't come with us today. But if I live I'll come back here. And then we'll figure out which one it'll be. I promise."

"I'll wait for you. I promise."

They gave each other a last squeeze then broke apart. She headed back out the main cargo hatch to resume her work.

Marcus looked about to see where things stood.

Alys sat in the crane operator booth, staring at him, her face expressionless.

He stared back. "Pick up that floater, spacer! Time is money."

***

The captain intended to do full maintenance checks on *Azure Tarn* after the loading was complete, then lift off in the morning. That was out the airlock with the rest of the plan. Welly, having less muscle than other crew, was on the bridge running diagnostics on all the systems she was qualified on.

"Um. Hello."

She pivoted to look at the hatch. Dilwyn stood there, looking uncertain what to do with his hands. He finally shoved one into a pocket and used the other prop himself on the coaming.

"Hi yourself. Coming along for the trip?"

"No. I asked permission to come aboard to, um, talk to you."

"All right." She waved him toward the helmsman's seat.

"Thank you, I won't be staying long. It's just—I'm sorry about all this trouble."

Ah. No last minute marriage proposal from Dilwyn. Well, a wanted criminal wouldn't be his style.

"It's all right. We knew we were breaking some rules."

"I'm glad you did. I mean, I'm glad you came here. I'm glad I met you."

"Me, too." Welly walked over to the hatch and wrapped her arms around him. He matched the hug, squeezing her tight, and leaned down for a kiss.

A pleasant kiss, but it didn't have the *intent* his kisses used to have.

"Thank you for saying good-bye," Welly said.

"Yes. Good bye. And good luck. With your trip. And . . . everything."

Too upright to even say, 'I hope you don't get arrested.' How was this stiff related to a rebel like Vychan?

She gave him a quick peck on the cheek. Dilwyn flashed a smile then turned away. His shoes rang down the corridor.

Welly went back to her console. The power storage diagnostic routine still had another minute to run. No errors yet.

***

Marcus took up the slack in the tie down strap then checked the time. He looked up. His father stood at the top of the forward stairs. "Captain," he called, "how are we doing on time?"

"Lift in eighteen minutes."

No change from the original timeline then. The front and aft ends of the hold were stuffed solid with vehicles stacked on top of each other. But there was no time for more of that.

"Secure crane," he ordered Alys. Then he turned to the Goch clansmen sitting in the driver's seats of the remaining vehicles. "No more stacking. Drive them all in."

Marcus emphasized this with waves of his arms.

A liftvan started forward. It headed for the fore corner of the bare deck in the hold. A flatbed headed aft. More vehicles followed.

The supercargo scrambled up on the stack of ytterbium ingots welded together in the center of the hold. More waves directed the enthusiastic drivers into the best fit.

More or less.

"Are you all right?" Marcus asked the driver of a two seater crunched between two trucks.

"I'm fine," replied Dilwyn Goch, scrambling out, "but that one's never lifting again."

"It's good for parts," said Marcus. He grabbed Dilwyn's hand to pull him up onto the relative safety of the ingots. More drivers joined them. They watched the scrum on the deck in fascination.

A youngster Marcus couldn't remember the name of pulled up next to the ingots in obedience to Marcus' gestures. He said, "I could pop this on top of there if you want to squeeze a few more in."

Seven minutes left.

"Okay, wait a minute and we'll do that." Marcus raised his voice. "All vehicles freeze!"

In a minute they were all stationary. Marcus turned to the others on the ingots. "Head out, grab a new ride."

They scampered out.

Marcus climbed onto the younger's flatbed. A crate filled most of the bed. He sat on top of it to check on the evacuation. Everyone was clear. "Go for it, kid."

The driver grinned and twisted his controls. The flatbed floater whined, lurched, and rose several feet into the air. It scraped over the top layer of ingots then lifted some more. A bit of wiggling slid it onto the stack with only a foot of the tail sticking out.

The faint high whine of the engine faded. A thump said the floater was at rest now. Marcus let go of the tie down holding the crate in place. He stood on the crate and addressed the next open top floater. "Can you fit that on the other side?"

The driver nodded and popped his up with less fuss than the first one.

"Last chance! Squeeze them in!" Marcus waved both arms, palms toward himself, to bring the floaters in.

A couple minutes of thumps, crunches, and curses filled the deck.

"If you're not on the crew it's time to get off!" Marcus stepped from vehicle to vehicle, urging drivers ahead of him. He hopped down onto the hatch, lowered into its ramp position.

Drivers were jumping into parked floaters and moving them away, then running back to get another.

Some weren't being moved far enough. "Move them outside the red circle!" Marcus ordered. He pointed at the painted stripe encircling the landing pad for anyone who didn't get it.

Wynny blew a kiss as she ran to a liftvan.

Marcus blew one back and hoped she saw it. Every floater was off the ramp. He told Alys to close the hatch.

Climbing over floaters was going to get him hurt sooner or later. But the deck was packed, there were hardly any places where he could reach it. Sometimes he'd moved around the hold on the crane hook. It wasn't a good time to ask Alys for that favor.

Metal screeched as the hatch crumpled two floaters parked over the hinges. The whole mass of vehicles was pushed closer together.

On the bright side, thought Marcus, *they'll be less likely to shift in turbulence now.*

***

On the bridge, the first mate looked up from the comm console. "Supercargo reports hold secure for lift."

"Good," said the captain. "Get us clearance. Immediate lift."

She switched to the spaceport ground frequency. "Control, *Azure*

Tarn requests permission to lift to filed flight plan. Yes, I know it was only filed half an hour ago, I filed it. Standing by."

After muting her headset the mate turned to the captain. "They hadn't checked with Orbital Traffic Control to find a window yet."

Landry chuckled. "Bureaucratic incompetence has done well for us here. I can't be too angry at them." He looked at the helmsman. "Bring all systems up for flight. I want to lift the instant we have clearance."

"Aye-aye," said Roger. His hands moved over the controls. The ship began to hum as the drives warmed up. Then shrill beeps cut across the noise. Red lights lit up on consoles across the bridge.

The helmsman slapped at switches. The alarms stopped.

Nothing happened for a long moment. Landry wondered if Roger was counting to ten.

Roger turned on his intercom mike. "There's a live antigrav source in the cargo hold. Please turn that off before we blow out an artificial gravity generator."

***

Marcus and Alys stared at the ceiling of the cargo hold as Roger's voice came from the PA speakers. They'd both reached the bottom of the aft stairs. He turned to look over the hold.

The stacks of vehicles in the aft end towered over him. They'd been packed up against the stairs. He could touch them. He did. No vibration.

Marcus looked up at Alys. "Get on the intercom. Ask if he can tell where it is."

She nodded and ran up the stairs.

He faced the rest of the hold. It must be one of the floaters on the deck. The others had been stacked with the crane. A live antigrav unit would have been noticed as Alys picked it up.

Marcus hopped on to the flatbed next to the stairs. His stomach tightened as he caught his balance before going face-first into a two-seater. He climbed on top of the flatbed's cab. That let him reach the top of a liftvan sitting next to it.

His heart sank surveying the mass of vehicles. Climbing over all them like this would take hours. He'd still be at it when the Censorials arrived to arrest them all.

"In the middle, toward port side," yelled Alys. She stood by the intercom panel at the top of the stairs.

The hatch they'd loaded through was on port side. It was probably one of the last ones loaded. Some driver was caught up in the frantic rush and afraid of being trapped in his floater. He'd jumped out without bothering to turn the key off.

Liftvan to passenger taxi to cargo truck to a family model. Marcus paused to catch his breath. He'd be safer doing this on hands and knees but that would slow him down. Better to stay on his feet and take the risk.

His work boots had good traction but the tops of vehicles weren't designed for people to walk on. The curved roof of a sedan dumped Marcus off. He landed in the bed of a cargo hauler, the low wall smashing into his hip hard enough to make him see stars.

After snarling a string of curses he braced his hand on a crate, staggered to his feet, and jumped to the next one. This one had braces on the back of the cab, making it easy to climb on top. Metal squeaked as it bent under his weight.

Marcus studied the floaters close to the hatch. A family model caught his eye. It sat higher than the others of the same type, canted at an angle between two trucks. He started toward it.

Now he was climbing over the ones crunched by the closing hatch. He tripped on a ridge in the roof of a smushed taxi. He detoured to use three sturdy trucks as a path to his target. They looked safer to walk on than the damaged smaller ones.

Peeking into the windows of his target showed glowing readouts on the dashboard. It was still turned on. Hopefully it was the only one. The tabs showed the doors were unlocked.

Pulling on them proved the floater was wedged too tightly for the doors to open. Marcus braced himself against the truck and pushed with his feet against the floater's frame. Nothing moved.

He considered going back for a toolkit. His imagination supplied

Censorial troops knocking on the hatch. Breaking in with his bare hands wasn't an option . . . but his boots had metal toes.

Swinging his leg from the hip produced a crack through the middle of the window. A few more kicks created a spiderweb. The metal in the boot kept his toes unharmed. The rest of his foot was aching from the impacts.

A last hard kick shattered the window. A sweet smell escaped, some spray the seller used to cover mildew. His heel stomped on the shards sticking out of the frame. When the hole was big enough for him to fit through Marcus slid through feet first. A sting seared his thigh as a spike he'd missed sliced through pants and skin.

Marcus grabbed the key. Twisted. The dashboard went dark.

He stuck his head through the window and yelled, "Alys, check if we're good now."

She didn't answer. A minute later he felt the solid pull of planetary gravity replaced by the faint shimmy of an artificial gravity generator. Marcus let out a deep sigh. *We can lift now.*

He rubbed at a tickle on the inside of his knee. He put his head out the window again. "Can you bring the first aid kit?"

***

"All systems ready for lift," reported Roger.

"Thank you," said Captain Landry. He turned to the first mate. "Please ping Control again for our clearance."

While that conversation went on he looked out the bridge windows. No approaching Censorial troops yet.

"Acknowledged, Control, standing by." Lane pulled her headset off and cursed.

"No clearance?" asked the captain.

"Clearance denied. Traffic upstairs is too thick for a ship to pass through on this shift. I think they don't like being pushed for a quick response."

He thought for a moment. "Betty, warm up the dish."

"Huh? Oh, aye-aye." The sensor tech began the sequence for the main radar. Normally she watched through the secondary systems in supervised volumes. Traffic controllers didn't like strange pings blasting their sensitive receivers.

A few minutes later—no Censorials spotted yet—Betty reported, "Main radar dish ready, sir."

"Thank you. First mate, inform Control that we're lifting on our own responsibility to detect and avoid."

There was only a beat of silence before the mate said, "Yes, sir," and put the headset back on.

The rest of the bridge crew was silent during the brief conversation.

Lane pulled the headset off. "Okay, they're looking up the made-up regulation number I cited at them."

The captain said, "Helmsman, up ship!"

Roger slid the thrust levers forward. Through the windows they could see the port and city fall away.

The weather was clear. Winds didn't bother them. Once a few miles high they could see an approaching hurricane. It would have made lift off more interesting if they'd waited two days.

The first mate's hands flew over her dials as she eavesdropped on conversations in orbit. "There's a navigation hazard announcement on us. And several ships panicking over it. Requests for new trajectories and parking orbits."

"Can't see why," said Betty. "There's plenty of room around our trajectory."

Her display showed ships and space stations ahead of them. The curve of *Azure Tarn's* planned route to interplanetary space did not intercept any of their vectors.

The sky faded from blue to black as they rose out of Corwynt's atmosphere. Landry felt a sense of relief at escaping the world, even though the rational part of his mind knew they weren't free yet.

Betty reported, "Someone just evaded into our path." She linked the display to the repeaters at the other consoles.

"Shifting vector to port," said Roger. The curve moved to clear the projected position of the other ship.

"And another one," said Betty. "They're not even trying to avoid us. This is domino effect. They're trying to stay clear of others panicking."

Roger adjusted course again.

The captain had the repeater panel attached to his chair across his lap. He studied it. "Roger, abort the gravity turn. Head straight out on our current vector."

The helmsman looked back.

The captain met his look firmly.

Roger turned back and adjusted his controls. "Linear ascent, aye. That's going to take more fuel, sir."

"It sure will. But look at the radar display."

Everyone on the bridge turned to their repeaters. All the ships in orbit were moving away from the straight line trajectory.

"Dammit, I filed a lift plan with the gravity turn," said Lane.

"You did," agreed Landry. "But it was rejected so they didn't relay it to anyone."

"And they thought we were stupid enough to waste fuel on a linear ascent?" said Roger.

"The ones who panicked did."

***

Bundoran was an easy post for the Censorial Investigative Service. Anti-Censorial incidents were usually solved the same day. Here's the subject who assaulted a Censorial agent (execute). Here's the bureaucrat who screwed up enough to enrage him (reprimand). The investigators were home in time for dinner.

Superintendent Ping liked being in charge of the Bundoran CIS. He'd never be promoted but he was close enough to retirement to not care. His wife was already researching which worlds would give them the shortest travel time to their grandchildren.

His comm lit up. There went the day. "Superintendent Ping."

Commandant Feliz said, "You are ordered to arrest the crew of the merchant ship *Azure Tarn* by the Will of the Censor. All are to be interrogated thoroughly."

Ping stiffened. How could there be something meriting Will of the Censor in his city without him knowing? He said only, "I hear and obey, ma'am. They will be arrested at once."

"Good." The comm went dark.

It would be lovely to know what the spacers had done. Or what information the interrogators were supposed to find. But Ping knew better than to bother Feliz with questions. He'd talk to her staffers, or ask his friends at Planetary Headquarters. That would wait.

"Schmidt!" he yelled.

The adjutant popped into Ping's office. "Sir?"

"Get a squad. Then arrest—" Ping relayed the order.

"Yessir. Lethal force?"

"No, no. We want them all answering questions. And now that I think on it I'd wager there's a secret agent in the crew. How else would HQ know to arrest them?"

That made Schmidt thoughtful. "True. I wouldn't want to kill one of Secret Observation's pets. Bad for my career."

To be safe Schmidt called up two squads, the majority of the enlisted CIS had on day shift in the city. A quick meeting with the Chief Investigators leading each squad produced a plan. Briefing the plan and rules of engagement to the squads only took an hour. Then they loaded up in four armored liftvans and headed for the spaceport.

The weather was clear. Schmidt enjoyed the sea breeze. Fresh air was a rare thing when working in an arcology.

The only traffic moving on the spaceport was a mismatched line of floaters going past them into the city. Only half of them were loaded with cargo. No ships were moving. There were only a half dozen parked on the spaceport today. None looked like the image of the Azure Tarn found in the spaceport reports.

As planned the liftvans stopped in a circle around Landing Pad 26. The troops leapt out and formed lines between each pair of liftvans. It went perfectly despite not having time for a rehearsal.

The only problem was that Landing Pad 26 was empty.

Schmidt found the radio frequency for the spaceport control

center. "Control, where's the *Azure Tarn*? Your report said it was on twenty-six."

"Um, yessir," came the reply. "Sir, *Azure Tarn* lifted twelve minutes ago."

"Thank you," said Schmidt. He cursed. Now the promotion for catching them would go to some damn Space Traffic Control officer.

***

Soon went back to plotting courses. Her carefully calculated trajectory to the jump point went into the dumpster when the ship changed course. The captain clearly didn't care about saving fuel. The tanks were topped off. The display showed hardly any traffic over ten thousand clicks altitude. She set the course change there and projected a straight line flight to the jump point.

"Out of atmosphere, increasing acceleration," said Roger. A ripple went through the artificial gravity as it adjusted, quick enough the crew wondered if it was their imagination.

"Bundoran Spaceport Control has given up on us," said the first mate. "All the complaints are coming from Orbital Traffic Control now. We're ordered to maneuver to a parking orbit."

"Acknowledged," said the captain.

Betty cursed. "New bogey moving toward our path. Not a collision course. Extrapolating the curve . . . will be paralleling us at a hundred clicks."

"Transponder code?" asked the captain.

"Checking." Betty tapped on her console. "OTC cutter five."

That made some of the crew flinch. Betty wasn't bothered. She seemed pleased that her doomsaying would finally come to pass.

"We expected official attention," said Landry. "Let's hope they don't have permission to do anything yet."

After a moment's thought he activated the intercom. "Marcus, go to my cabin and get some jewelry out of the safe. Nothing sentimental. The big fancy pieces."

***

Alys tagged along. Marcus didn't object. It wasn't like there was any work she could do. He didn't let her follow him into his parent's cabin.

When he emerged she whistled low and long. "Pretty. What's it for?"

"Captain didn't say. I'm guessing we may try to bribe an inspector."

"Wow. Um—all that?"

Marcus shrugged. "I don't know. Mr. Goch had stories of bribing Censorials to get cargos through. But traffic violations are different."

***

"Crap." Lane put the radio on speaker.

"Control Cutter to merchant *Azure Tarn*. You are in violation of orbit traffic control regulations. Cut thrust and prepare to be boarded."

"Cut me in," said Landry.

She flipped a few switches and flashed a thumbs up.

"Cutter, this is Captain Landry of the *Azure Tarn*. I apologize for violating regulations. We have a customer needing an urgent delivery. I accept paying the appropriate fine." He put a note of humor in his voice. "The fine will be charged to our customer for demanding rapid delivery."

"*Azure Tarn*, cut thrust and prepare to be boarded. If you continue to flee you will be fired upon."

"Cutter, this doesn't have to become violent. I'm perfectly willing to have a hearing over radio, or report in person after delivering our cargo."

"*Azure Tarn*, cut thrust. We will target your propulsion system but cannot guarantee there will be no injury to crew."

The bridge crew tensed and exchanged looks.

"Cutter, I will need written documentation of your demand to show to my customer."

"*Azure Tarn*, there will be plenty of paperwork." Was the Censorial officer smiling as he said that? No way to be sure. "Cut thrust and prepare to be boarded."

"We understand and will comply." Landry made a throat-cutting gesture.

The first mate muted the microphone.

Roger was already looking over his shoulder, hand on the thrust controls.

"Cut thrust," the captain ordered. Another barely detectable shiver went through the artificial gravity.

"It's maneuvering to rendezvous," reported Betty.

Landry stood. "Can I see it from here?"

Betty needed a moment to relate her display to the bridge windows. "Almost. It's just past the port window." She pointed to the bulkhead behind the communications console.

"Roger, yaw ten degrees port."

The helmsman had a gentle touch with the thrusters. It felt like they were holding still and the stars outside shifted around the ship.

"There it is." Betty pointed at a moving dot near the edge of the window.

"Hand me the monocular," said Landry.

He focused the viewer on the cutter. It was a round ended cylinder, almost hidden under racks and pylons holding equipment of various sorts. Most looked to be search and rescue gear. There were four missiles on extendible pylons. They hadn't been bluffing.

Landry lowered the monocular. "It's a vacuum buggy," he said with satisfaction.

The cutter commander's voice came across the speaker again. "*Azure Tarn*, I'm not familiar with your design. Where's your personnel airlock?"

Landry turned to the first mate. "Send them to the port dorsal lock. Have Marcus open the outer door."

Then he went back to thinking.

As the cutter closed in, he ordered, "Roger, stand by to execute a maximum power plus yaw and plus pitch on my command."

The helmsman protested, "Sir, that will—"

"Set it up and execute at my command!"

"Yessir!" Roger was more surprised than scared. Landry hadn't shown anger at him before. He positioned the thruster controls.

The cutter was visible to the naked eye now. It decelerated to make a gentle docking. The mechanical protrusions made it look like a sea urchin or spiky crab.

Azure Tarn could accelerate to almost the speed of light in normal space. In practice her top speed was limited by the need to spend as much time decelerating as accelerating before arriving at her destination.

In atmosphere or hyperspace her speed was constrained by the strength of her hull. The resistance of the medium went up by the square of her speed. At sea level on Corwynt she could only go Mach Ten. Any faster risked rupturing her hull. A few weak points had been reinforced by previous owners.

A ship which only traveled in interplanetary space—a 'vacuum buggy' to snobbish interstellar spacers—only needed a hull strong enough to hold in the crew's air and support whatever was mounted on the outside. Maintenance personnel needed to be careful not to make accidental punctures when swinging tools about.

As the cutter extended its docking tube Landry snapped, "Roger, now!"

The helmsman slammed two levers to their maximum.

Azure Tarn's artificial gravity generators were networked with the thrusters. They kept the crew from feeling most of the pivot by compensating for the expected forces.

The impact with the cutter wasn't predicted. They all felt the lurch as the ship slammed against the smaller vessel. Worse was the sound, the crunch of crumpled metal, screech of wreckage scraping over the hull, and wail of alarms.

On the bridge they could see the wreck spin away. "Belay rotation," ordered Landry. "Full thrust for the jump point."

"Aye-aye." Roger scrambled to obey. The full power of the main drive was more than the AG could compensate for. They all felt the deck tilted up toward the bow.

Landry watched the wrecked cutter. All the attachments from one side were expanding debris. The hull was in one piece. The cracks were large enough no more air was escaping. One of the exterior lights was blinking red.

"Is it transmitting anything?" he asked Lane.

"Automated distress signal, Hold on." She listened to her headset. "New message. Same guy who was talking to us. Requests assistance."

"Thanks." So there was at least one survivor. If anyone hadn't been suited up when Landry rammed them they were dead now. Whatever the original arrest order was for, Landry now faced arrest for murder or an act of war.

As *Azure Tarn* accelerated away the wreckage fell out of sight.

"Turn off the transponder," ordered Landry. No sense pretending to be a law-abiding ship.

***

"Governor? Do you have a moment?"

Bridge Yeager looked up from his reader. Whatever his aide was bringing to him had to be more interesting than the Censorate Council's latest update to the Index of Prohibited Ideas. He locked the reader. The Index was at the maximum level of security. "Certainly, Benno. What is it?"

"Director Yokat and Director Pellel wish to see you. They say it's urgent."

"Send them in."

Benno led the directors in. His offer of refreshment was cut short by a glare from Yokat. The Director of Order waved the aide out the door, shoving it closed just shy of the poor man's foot.

Then Yokat took his place next to his fellow director.

Yeager studied them. Neither was interested in the soft chairs before the desk. They were almost at attention. It felt as if they were expecting to be chastised. He raised his eyebrows to invite them to begin.

Director Yokat spoke. "Your excellency, I have failed to carry out your order."

Censorial governors possessed the authority to execute a subordinate on the spot for such lapses. Some did. Yeager asked, "Which order?"

"I did not arrest and interrogate the crew of the *Azure Tarn*. They fled the planet before my team arrived."

"I see. So you requested Director Pellel apprehend them in space?"

Pellel took a quarter-step forward. "No, sir. My people attempted to seize the ship for multiple violations of traffic control regulations. The criminals rammed the inspection cutter. Destroyed it."

"How are the crew?" demanded Yeager.

"They'll recover. Broken bones, vac bite, a concussion. Fortunately they were all suited up for the boarding. But all my available cutters were needed to rescue the casualties. The *Azure Tarn* was out of range before we could spare one to go after them."

To his surprise Yeager's reaction was relief. He'd ordered the arrest in a fit of anger after being lied to. In the morning he'd wondered if he'd overreacted to an honest error. Now there was proof these visitors were ruthless traitors, with information sources inside his own administration. His order had been correct.

"I see," said the governor. "What authorization do you need to pursue them?"

Yokat answered, "Neither of our directorates can reach the ship now. We, um, suggest that naval assistance be requested."

Yeager tapped his fingers on the desktop as he thought. In his years as governor he'd avoided calling in the military. Mowing down rioters or bombarding a city struck him as a failure of leadership, not an exercise of it. But a fleeing spaceship was certainly a task for the Navy.

"Very well." He pressed the switch to open the door and raised his voice. "Benno!"

The aide appeared in the doorway. "Sir?"

"Find out if the Commodore is on world. If so, get him on the line."

"Yessir." Benno vanished. A moment later he returned. "On your screen, sir."

The center of Yeager's desk lit up with the face of Commodore

Meckler. He wore a deferential smile, an expression which sat uncomfortably on a visage accustomed to demanding unhesitating obedience. "Governor Yeager. How may I serve your excellency?"

"We have a problem which seems best solved by the Navy. A ship of traitors has fled Corwynt and is beyond our power to catch." Yeager summarized *Azure Tarn's* escape. "I hope dealing with them is within the Navy's power."

He'd carefully worded his speech to avoid any orders or demands. While the naval squadron did have orders to assist civilian authorities, the commodore could appeal any order he didn't like to his admiral at district headquarters, adding at least a month's delay. Yeager was thankful he'd invited the obnoxious bastard to a dinner or gala at least monthly.

The commodore grinned. "I wager the boys would enjoy some target practice. Don't have the budget for much live fire rounds these days."

"Certainly. Traitors deserve no better. But we do have a long list of questions for them if there could be survivors." A longer list than when Yeager first ordered their interrogation.

"That takes some of the fun out of it. And it's harder than just blowing them up. But a challenge is good for the boys. Let me see which ship has the ready duty." The seal of the Censorial Navy replaced the commodore's face.

Yeager waited patiently. Neither director offered a comment.

Commodore Meckler reappeared. "Good news, Governor. The carrier *Implacable* is on duty. She can head after them as soon as I send the orders. Which I'll do now."

"Thank you, Commodore."

The screen went blank. It was just as well Meckler hadn't tried to add some pleasantries to the conversation. He wasn't any good at it.

Yeager looked at his subordinates. "Director Pellel. Please inform me of the recovery of your casualties. Director Yokat. You will provide daily reports on your progress toward finding out how the traitors were warned of my arrest order."

Both men bowed.

"Dismissed."

***

Captain Wing sipped his tea. Thirty hours of standing at alert with no work to do made staying awake a struggle. A normal shift would have maintenance, training, or an exercise. As ready ship *Implacable* couldn't do any of those, lest it interfere with their ability to react instantly.

"Skipper, message from the Flag. New orders." The yeoman held out a message pad.

"Good. I've been telling the Commodore's staff we should have exercises for the ready ship."

"No, sir. It's a real mission. Pursuit and capture."

Wing snatched the pad, shoving the tea cup into the yeoman's hands.

"Well, well. Looks like we're cleaning up a mess for our civilian colleagues. Helm!"

The bridge crew had all woken from their bored daze at the captain's reaction. "Sir?" acknowledged the helmsman.

"Maximum thrust at course, hmmm, 140 by 60. We'll refine that in a few minutes. Navigator, take a look at this. Give me a rendezvous."

The carrier swung toward deep space. She was orbiting Glogfaen, next world out from Corwynt. It was a boring rock which no one minded the Navy bombing for practice, other than the rare miners or reclusive settlers.

Wing took his tea back to distract himself from breathing down his navigator's neck. The boy knew his trade. There was no sense distracting him.

"Sir, we can't do it. It has too big a head start on us. I can't even pull off a fly-by intercept before it reaches that jump point."

Wing suppressed a curse.

"The fighters can reach it," continued the navigator. "They can be at the jump point waiting for it."

"Thank you." Wing turned to his XO. "Scramble Squadron Two."

"Aye, sir!" In minutes the vacuum-specialized fighters were shooting into space.

***

"Stand by for turnover," said Soon. She watched the timer count down. "Execute turnover."

"Executing," said Roger. Stars swept by the windows of the bridge as he flipped *Azure Tarn* end for end.

The crew felt fine. The artificial gravity was prepared to compensate for the pivot. It kept them from feeling any vibrations.

Even better, this marked the halfway point in their flight to hyperspace. Twelve more hours and they could say goodbye to this system. Shoulders unkinked.

"We're being pinged," said Betty. "Not Corwynt Traffic Control this time. Different frequency."

Landry turned to face her. He didn't demand more details. Her hands were moving briskly across the sensor console. When she had more information she'd share it.

"It's a fancy ping," Betty continued. "Multiple pulses at different frequencies. Permission to ping them back? The source is in the main dish's field of view."

"Granted."

Whatever was interested in them, it wasn't close. It took several minutes for the response—responses—to come back.

Betty described the readouts as they came in. "Whoa, that's bright. Corner reflector strength. Must be vacuum buggies with gear all over them again. Coming at us fast, there's some blue-shift on the echoes. Looks like ten of them in two lines. Ah, another echo lagging behind them. Dimmer, probably a smooth hull. The mother ship I'd guess."

She paused, then laughed. "Oh, Momma has her transponder turned on. How peacetime of them. Let's see who we're dealing with. 'SCSH-3492, CNS *Implacable.*' Then a bunch of letters that mean nothing to me. But it looks like a carrier and a bunch of fighters heading straight toward us."

"Can you estimate their speed?" asked the captain.

"No. I'll ping them again in an hour, that should be enough of a delta to let me calculate their acceleration."

The relaxation on the bridge had vanished. The crew were all hunched with tension. Except for Betty, who'd been expecting disaster and seemed to welcome it.

The other effect of the Navy pursuit was to ruin Landry's plan for resting his crew. Once past turnover he'd planned to put the ship on half manning. Instead everyone wanted to stay up to see the result of Betty's next ping.

Marcus took over the power console, well rested after a post-loading nap and fresh bandage. That forced Welly to go off duty. Lane went to their cabin, but a text message demanding updates made it clear she wasn't sleeping. Everyone else insisted they were needed at their post.

Hints from Roger and Soon persuaded Betty that fifty minutes was enough of an increment to calculate the vectors. When the echoes finally came back Soon copied the data to her console to do the projections.

"Shit." Soon turned to face her expectant audience. "They'll be at the jump point ten minutes before us."

"Well . . . damn." Landry castigated himself for not showing proper confidence in front of the crew. Then again, confidence wouldn't help this situation much.

"What do we do?" asked Soon.

"Might be time to surrender," offered Betty.

Roger snarled, "You think they won't execute you, bitch?"

"Lock it up," ordered the captain.

Marcus studied Soon's plot on his repeater screen. "We could stop decelerating," he offered. "We don't have to be stationary when we transition."

"Yeah, if we don't mind being ripped to bits," said Roger.

"Lots of ships have done fast transitions. It'll be rough but beats a Censorial torture cell."

"Or they'll put a missile into us when they figure out what we're up to," said Betty. "Guess that's still better than torture."

Landry turned to his son, an inquiring look on his face.

"If it looked like a drive failure they wouldn't shoot," said Marcus thoughtfully. "They'd wait for the carrier to catch up and take us in tow."

"That could work," said the captain. "Let's talk to Gander about faking a failure. Soon, you have the con."

***

Marcus normally didn't mind the fit of his spacesuit. It was snug, but that was a necessary part of keeping him alive and functioning. He just wished it could be adjusted for unusual conditions. Such as a bandage on his thigh being compressed into the wound.

Well, it didn't hurt much. Not enough to slow him down. At least he wasn't going to slow down in front of Alys and Tets. They were helping him with his part of the fake-an-engine-failure plan: tossing three floaters overboard to simulate debris from a drive explosion.

They'd rigged the floaters to explode before depressurizing the hold. Delicate electronics work was bad enough without doing it in pressure gloves. Though it wasn't that delicate. These weren't space rated units. Operating outside a gravity field they'd tear themselves to pieces. Marcus and Tets were just splicing out the regulators which would shut the process down.

They concentrated on not making the floaters explode in the cargo hold.

Alys, not having electronics training, was operating the crane. She'd expanded her experience by pulling floaters loose from the jam next to the hatch. Having one pull loose and bounce off the overhead was not in the crane operator's guide. But she'd gotten it back under control and placed by the main cargo hatch to be sabotaged.

Now they were watching the countdown to the thrust cut-off. There'd been no way to estimate how fast a transition the ship could handle. Soon calculated when they'd have to stop decelerating to evade the fighters. They'd go through to hyperspace at that speed, live or die.

Three floatcars lay on their sides on top of others, tops facing the hatch. Marcus and Tets stood by them. Their safety lines were tied to girders overhead.

The artificial gravity turned off. Marcus felt his arms float up toward their natural position. That meant the drive was off, or they'd be slammed against the aft bulkhead. Alys started opening the main cargo hatch. The motors were sized to close it against three gravities. There were large warning labels declaring that excessive speed in low gravity could cause major damage. Marcus had told Alys, "Open and close it *fast*. We can fix it later."

The hatch was fully open in seconds. Marcus grabbed the antigrav car and kicked hard against the liftvan they'd been resting on. Once they were a few feet clear he reached in through the open driver's window and pressed the start button.

The car pushed away from the ship, resisting the pull of a planet it didn't realize wasn't there.

The fringe of the antigrav field pushed Marcus away as it would any unlucky pedestrian. He twisted to land on his feet, making the wound in his thigh spasm again.

Marcus glanced at Tets. The mechanic had bounced away but looked unhurt. Marcus grabbed the third car, pressed the button, and pushed it off the truck it laid on.

He hurried, putting some spin on the car. That sent Marcus toward the overhead and the car glanced against the hatch on its way out.

Marcus transmitted, "Alys, close it."

The hatch began to move. A car flared white. Marcus' helmet rang as a fragment bounced off it.

"Tets, Alys, are you okay? Sound off."

She answered, "I'm fine."

The mechanic said, "Damn, I saw some shrapnel go right past me."

Marcus switched frequencies. "Bridge, they're clear. Initiate spin."

"Acknowledged," came his father's voice.

The stars visible past the closing hatch moved as the ship began to yaw.

Tets bumped into Marcus. The mechanic grabbed his arm. His

other hand laid a strip of vacctape on Marcus' faceplate.

"What the hell are you doing?"

"Sir, your helmet's cracked."

"No, it's not. It wasn't leaking."

"Let's keep it that way."

***

"Enemy closing in," said Betty.

"Acknowledged," replied Captain Landry. He'd been watching the fighters approach on the repeater screen. His initial fear they'd put a missile into his ship had faded. Now he was afraid they'd come close enough to check for damage and not find any.

Which could inspire a missile shot.

Azure Tarn was still in a gentle spin. Stars slid port to starboard in the windows. Streaks passing by were fighters shooting past them.

"Past first buoy," reported Soon.

In theory they could safely transition to hyperspace now. In practice . . . he wanted to be well clear of the shoals when making a rough transition.

Roger muttered, "They're not getting real close."

"After what we did to that cutter?" said Marcus. "I'm not surprised."

Betty smirked. "You're getting your wish. One's accelerating to match our velocity."

Landry looked up from the repeater. There it was. A lean, vicious version of the cutter. A pressure hull just big enough for one pilot. A powerful thruster. Many pylons supporting missiles, cannon, radar and lidar transmitters, and other devices he couldn't identify. He was sure their purpose was violence.

The fighter drifted out of sight as the ship spun. Now the pilot was looking at the undamaged engines. And reporting his observations to his commander.

Landry pressed the intercom switch. "Chief, take us through."

Then his chair twisted out from under him. He rolled across the deck, flailing in search of something to hold on to. Pain shot through his shoulder as he slammed into the base of a chair. He grabbed it with both hands, feeling its immobility. His body twisted in the belief the deck was falling away.

The bridge was lit only by the glow of hyperspace shoals coming through the windows. At least two crew were vomiting. One screamed. A whiff of smoke cut through the vomit odor. A string of pops told of circuits burning as wild energy made it past the breakers.

The vertigo started to fade. Holding on tight let the hands outvote the ears. Landry took a deep breath. Lying on the deck was safe. Restful. He was due for some rest.

The occupant of the chair retched. There was splatter on the deck. One drop hit Landry's hand. He began pulling himself up the back of the chair.

Nobody else was on the deck. The screaming had stopped. There was plenty of cursing. The emergency lights were on but couldn't compete with the light from outside.

Landry looked out the window. *Azure Tarn* was still spinning. There was no fog present. He could see the shoals clearly. As the ship turned the near shoals came into view.

Judging distance in hyperspace depended on the blurriness induced by the layers of aether between viewer and target. That shoal looked crisp.

"Roger, are the thrusters responding?" Landry shouted over the noise.

The helmsman was sitting upright in his chair. His hands hovered, barely touching the controls. "Dunno. The jump messed up my vision extra hard. All I can see is neon shapes moving around."

The near shoals came into view again. The cumulus-like surface looked a little different from the last look. Were they getting closer?

The captain moved to the helm. He kept his feet braced on the deck when he shifted a hand from chair to chair. He was in no shape to take an unsupported step. When he had both hands on the back of Roger's chair he asked, "What can you see now?"

"I can make out the window frame."

Landry discarded the thought of taking over the position. He was too wobbly to operate the thrusters. Roger's hands were steady. The boy just couldn't judge the effect of his actions. *Time to play seeing-eye captain.*

"Okay. Give me some plus yaw."

Roger twisted two levers in opposite directions. There was no change in the drift of the shoals outside. A promontory filled more of the sky than on the last rotation. Yes, they were drifting toward the shoals.

"Belay. It's not working." Landry raised his voice. "I need power to the thrusters."

At the power operator console, Marcus lowered the cloth he'd been wiping his mouth with. "We have power for antigrav, controls, and life support. The breakers went on everything else. I'm still tracing the faults."

"Give me thrusters even if you have to cut the rest."

"Aye-aye." There was too much noise to hear what Marcus did. Landry knew he'd been obeyed when his feet lifted off the deck.

The decades of spaceflight to become a captain-owner left Landry immune to ordinary space-sickness. Freefall plus lingering vertigo and the stench of other crew's failure to control their stomachs . . . was a challenge. Landry spread his feet wide and clamped onto the back of Roger's chair with all four limbs.

Once secure he said, "Try again, Roger."

The helmsman worked his controls. The promontory slowed its drift across the bridge windows.

"It's working! Give me some more. Good. Okay, cut thrust, but be ready to zero the spin when we're pointed at open space."

Roger started. "We're headed toward a shoal?"

"We have time. We're good. Minus yaw now."

The helmsman obediently applied the thrusters.

"Okay, get ready to cut it off . . . now. Good! Acceleration dead ahead."

The near shoal was now only visible in the starboard windows, receding. It glowed as lightning flashed inside the clouds. Roger was looking from side to side, making out some of the features of local hyperspace.

"Sir, we need some time for repair," said Marcus.

"Right. Betty, how long until that carrier can come through?"

"Four hours to reach the jump point," she said. "Plus however long she needs to load up her fighters."

His command chair wasn't far away, but Landry doubted he could aim himself at it accurately. He reached over Roger to take his intercom microphone and pressed the PA switch. "All hands. We will heave to for one hour to make repairs then resume travel at best speed."

He handed the mike back. "Roger, cut thrust. We're clear of the shoals on both sides."

The essential repairs took less than the full hour. Power, antigravity, and controls all tested green. Marcus then asked for all hands to help in the hold.

Captain Landry decided to take a look at the cargo hold before endorsing that. It was an impressive sight. He was tempted to photograph it for the supercargo instructors. He'd never seen worse.

"The problem was how squeezed they were," Marcus explained. "It was like compressing a spring. Gravity held them to the deck. When we turned it off, well, this."

All the floaters once parked on the deck of the hold were drifting through the air. Some were moving faster, bouncing off others or a bulkhead with loud rings. Crates brought aboard on flatbeds were now spinning on their own. Smaller objects told of crates broken open or floaters shedding pieces in collisions.

"So what's your plan?" asked the captain.

Marcus didn't hesitate. "Turn the AG on at one percent. Use the crane to shift any unstable stacks. Then run tie downs and nets over everything. That's what I want the help with."

"What about the loose parts?" Landry pointed at a half-empty crate bouncing off the secured stack of vehicles.

In free fall a shrug moved Marcus' whole body. "That'll have to wait. We're going to be chasing after them until we unload."

The hour ended with only a third of the loose floaters even partially tied down. Captain Landry left Tets to help Marcus and Alys finish the job. The rest of the crew reported to their stations.

Betty had stood watch while the rest labored in the hold. When they entered the bridge she reported, "No transitions or events, sir."

"Thank you," said the captain. "Roger, let's get underway."

"Aye-aye." The helmsman applied thrust, starting the ship along the course Soon had marked.

The navigator monitored his vector. "Mind the navigation buoy," she said.

"No, don't. Ram it," said Landry.

"Sir?" asked a confused Roger.

"It might be recording our movements," Landry explained. The leadership classes he'd taken said not to explain orders, but this wasn't the Navy. He needed their willing cooperation.

"Oh, okay." Roger shifted course toward the buoy.

The first mate said, "Don't hit it with the leading edges."

"Aye-aye, ma'am." As the buoy, an antenna-studded cube, filled the forward windows Roger pitched the ship up.

Azure Tarn's belly slammed into the buoy. Floating stationary in hyperspace didn't require a sturdy hull. The buoy's outer shell was thin as a vacuum buggy's. Unlike a vacuum buggy, it was a solid mass of electronics and batteries. The sound of it smashing against the hull rang through the ship.

In vacuum fragments just bounced off. The aether resisting *Azure Tarn's* passage held the buoy debris against the hull, scraping along until it slid past the stern. Which made for more noises spacers didn't like hearing.

"We're going to need a lot of repairs when we get to port," said Lane.

The captain growled, "As long as we get there we can replace the whole damn hull."

Betty sat up. "I have the signal of the next navigation buoy."

"Fine. If that's on the way to Fwynwr Ystaen we'll wreck that one too."

***

Captain Wing did not hover at the shoulder of his Fighter Operations Leader. Free-fall recovery operations were tricky. Cutting corners led to dead pilots, damaged carriers, and unpromotable captains.

So he sat on the bridge paging through reports while eavesdropping on the chatter as each fighter was tucked gently back into its socket. Recovering the pilots and leaving the fighters for their return to the system would have saved most of an hour but violated doctrine. A doctrine violation would be far worse for Wing's career than letting some mangy rebels escape to hide on some rock until their life support failed.

So he waited. And imagined blowing the freighter's drive apart to repay the false failure with a real one. One of the techs on the bridge had laughed out loud when the rebels jumped out. They would pay for that humiliation.

"Bird is seated. We have umbilical connection," reported a tech.

The Fighter Operations Leader pivoted to face Wing. "Sir, all fighters aboard."

Captain Wing sprang to his feet. "Engineering, transition to hyperspace!" Then he turned to the FOL. "Thank you, Lead."

The carrier's systems were built to handle even rough transitions. The only visible effect of transition was viewscreens blacking out then showing a view of hyperspace. Wing scented sugar, as if cotton candy was being shoved up his nose. A glance around the bridge showed no one bothered by transition effects. Of course, no one qualified for bridge duty without a dozen or more transitions.

"Barometry probes away, sir," said the sensor tech. He'd been thoroughly briefed on the need for prompt action.

Starting the survey promptly didn't reduce the time to produce an answer. Wing paged through more reports. He was certain his show of unconcern wasn't fooling anyone.

It took over ten minutes for the result. Wing knew it would be bad news. Anything useful would have been found sooner than that.

"Sir, we've found no aether wake. They must have left the area at least two hours ago. Also, the navigation buoy has been destroyed."

No surprise. "Lead, launch Squadron One, execute search as planned. Navigation, check which buoys we're getting signals from. Engineering, rig some replacement buoys. Something that will last long enough for Survey Corps to come out and clean up after these vandals."

The orders propagated down each chain of command, leaving Captain Wing with nothing to do but look calm again.

The first fighter launched in a pleasing seven minutes. It flashed across the view, a lean dart of a vehicle, optimized for penetrating air or aether. *Find those bastards*, thought Wing. *Cripple them. I want to watch them pay.*

***

Soon's meticulous records of their first trip, combined with the signals of the navigation buoys, let *Azure Tarn* make her way swiftly though the shoals surrounding Corwynt's star. Roger held the ship at a different angle when smashing each buoy to spread out the damage to the hull.

Betty shifted her attention from the view outside to her readouts. "I'm picking up some signals."

The captain pivoted toward her. "Radar or comm?"

"Dunno. It's too scrambled. Might be a mix of both. It's right at the edge of detectability. Probably bounced off multiple shoals before reaching us."

Welly had resumed her post at the power console. "They're still chasing us," she said. Then she flushed as she realized she'd spoken aloud.

Landry spoke in a reassuring tone. "We have a good head start. They may not even realize which way we went."

The signals were still faint when *Azure Tarn* emerged from the shoals. They flew through the phoenix formation, headed for the star where they'd first contacted humans outside the Fieran Bubble. Soon had no trouble keeping them on track. She'd taken pictures of all the hyperspace landmarks regularly on the outbound trip. She aimed Roger right at the rift they'd emerged from.

"On course and speed for next leg," reported Roger.

"Good," acknowledged the captain. "Let's pick up some more speed."

"How fast, sir? We're already halfway through the yellow zone." The helm console included a gauge measuring the aether pressure on the hull. If the needle reached red they could expect the hull to give way.

"Accelerate gradually. Let's see how she handles it. The designers always build some margin in. This is a good time to use it."

"Aye-aye." Roger nudged the thrust levers forward. The ship's drive only used its full capability in vacuum, when the ship could accelerate with the only limit being the artificial gravity's ability to counter the effect on the crew.

The needle moved through the rest of the yellow without any alarming groans or shudders from the hull. The bridge was silent, everyone's ears straining.

"Red now, sir," said Roger.

"Noted," said Landry.

Nothing was complaining. Welly watched her systems. A leak of aether into the ship could short out power lines. All the lines along the forward hull were functioning.

"I have warning alerts," said Betty. "It's the base of the main dish. The alignment motors are overloaded."

The captain said, "Acknowledged. Back off speed slightly."

Roger reduced thrust one notch, then two.

"No warnings," said Betty.

"Very well. Maintain this speed." Landry wished they'd dismounted the dish. It was designed to be folded up and fit through the cargo hold hatch. They'd cruise faster that way. But it would take hours of work to accomplish. They couldn't spare the time.

The worst part of being between stars was that they were fully visible to anything that might see them. Landry had considered bypassing this star, going around it to make a straight run back to the Bubble in open space. But that route had no place to hide. The shoals around the mining station's star were the best place to shake off their Censorial pursuit.

Especially if they could disappear into the rift before any Censorials emerged from the shoals around Corwynt's sun.

Landry was actually hoping they'd escaped by the time they were found.

Betty cursed. "Pings! High frequency. Definitely strong enough to get an echo off us. If they're close enough to ping us that hard they probably have a visual as well."

Reactions ranged from more curses to a whimper.

"We'll have a couple more chances to break contact," said the captain. He could only think of one, but maintaining morale was his duty.

"Multiple sources," Betty continued. "Identical transmitters. Simple pings. I'd bet these are from small craft. The mother ship is lagging behind, maybe looking at a different route."

"We can hope," Landry answered. Then he cursed himself. Sarcasm was no way to keep up his crew's confidence.

Another radar source registered on Betty's console before they reached the rift. "This one is lower frequency," she reported. "Likely from a larger vessel."

"The mother ship," said Landry grimly.

The entrance to the rift was wide. Roger had plenty of clearance to each side. "Sir, I'm reducing speed. Aether density is higher here."

"Acknowledged," answered Landry.

Once they'd been on course for the rift Soon had started a new project. Now she copied a plot to all the repeaters on the bridge. "Here's our course for the Fwynwr Ystaen system. I'll have to adjust it for where we actually emerge. This takes us to the entry point for the homeward channel in minimum time. We'll transition at sixty percent of the speed we did last time. I found a manual that says transition effects follow a square law, so it should only be a third as bad."

Faces tightened but no one objected to the plan.

Captain Landry did some quick calculations to check the timeline. "Good. If we can get through to the other passage before the Censorials transition into normal space they won't know where we went. They might even think we're hiding on a rock in the system."

That produced some hope. Roger actually smiled.

The smile vanished when Betty picked up a pair of pursuing fighters. "They're not closing on us very fast."

"Too small," said Landry. "In thin aether they're fast but they bog down in the thick stuff. Probably ran ahead of their mother ship in the gap."

"How well do missiles work?" asked Welly.

"In soup like this? Not at all. They'd have to come to kissing range and lase us." Landry ran some calculations. "Won't catch us in time."

As promised, the fighters were still out of attack range when *Azure Tarn* transitioned into the Fwynwr Ystaen system. The ship made no transmissions. It would be a poor return for the good deal the miners gave them to drag them into this mess.

The cruise across the system was simple enough Landry sent crew for naps again. He even took one himself.

Or he'd intended to. When Lane woke him he'd finished a full night's sleep, seven whole hours. "I set an alarm for three hours," he complained.

"I know. I turned it off," answered his wife. "You needed the rest."

She smirked as he bit his tongue to stifle more useless complaints. He asked, "Who has the con?" instead.

"Marcus. He's fully qualified and he needs more bridge time."

"All right." Landry staggered to the head, dealt with the essentials, and threw some water on his face. He looked longingly at the shower sack but there wasn't time for that before the transition back to hyperspace.

"Did you sleep any?" he asked Lane.

"Three hours and a bit. Marcus just woke me."

"Okay." He pulled on a working uniform, his rank indicated only by some embroidery on the shoulder of the shirt. The chest bore only his name and the ship's, same as any other member of the crew.

Marcus was sitting in the command chair when his parents arrived on the bridge. He cocked his head interrogatively at his father. Landry nodded. Marcus stood, declaring, "Captain has the con."

The captain took his seat. Everyone else was at their post already. His repeater screen held a helpful list of how much everyone had slept in the past 24 hours. "Helm, status?"

Roger, who'd also had a full seven hours, reported, "On track for transition."

"Thank you." A countdown showed on the repeater. Just over ten minutes.

Everyone was looking better. Sleep was part of it. They'd all been frayed around the edges by the stress of escaping. The larger share was the optimism. Nobody was actually *cheerful* but the worry and despair was fading.

Five minutes to transition.

Two minutes.

"Oh—" Betty's voice froze, as if she was searching for an appropriate expletive and couldn't find one strong enough. "Oh, heck. We've been pinged."

The rest of the crew found curses easily enough.

"It's the big transmitter again. Mamma must have followed us through."

Landry's voice was stern. "Focus on the jump. Worry about the Censorate later."

"We'll be through before the echo reaches them," said Betty.

The transition was executed on schedule. As Soon predicted it was about a third as rough. Which was still damn unpleasant.

Landry clung to the arms of his command chair, which pressed firmly against his butt in defiance of his ears' insistence that it was falling away and throwing him into a spin.

By the time he recovered enough to check on the crew, Soon had verified Roger's view of the shoals. The ship was homeward bound along the passage.

***

"No debris found," reported the sensor chief.

"They made a successful transition," said Captain Wing. "Follow them through."

"No, sir," said the astrogator.

Wing was too astonished to be angry. "Would you care to expand on that, Lieutenant Commander?"

The officer swallowed. "Of course, sir. Transitioning into hyperspace through untested coordinates is a Survey Corps responsibility. Survey always tests new points by transitioning from hyperspace to normal space to reduce the chance of a fatal collision. Navy doctrine on emergency transitions dictates that a pinnace or frigate must go through and return before hazarding a larger vessel."

The astrogator stood at parade rest, awaiting his fate.

"That is why you will not obey my order?" asked Captain Wing mildly.

"Yes, sir."

The captain turned to the assistant astrogator. "Lieutenant Gossem!"

"Yessir!" The junior officer was not happy to be noticed during this confrontation.

"Can you plot a jump where the freighter went through?"

"Um, yes, sir."

"Sir, he's willing," broke in the senior astrogator, "but the data he has to work with are a single radar fix and low resolution visual observations. That's far too large an error box to go through safely."

The captain's only response to this was, "You are relieved." Then he turned to the junior officer again. "Acting Lieutenant Commander Gossem, take us through."

"Yes, sir!" The joy of promotion was clear in Gossem's voice. Even if Wing couldn't make it permanent, time acting at a higher rank could take a year or two off the wait for promotion.

The executive officer approached Captain Wing. "Sir, this is reckless. If you intend to go through with the jump, I must also ask to be relieved."

"Very well, you are relieved. You may report to your quarters." Wing turned to the FOL. "Lead, you are acting XO."

***

The bridge was quiet as they slipped through the passage. The glowing pastel pink shoals on each side lit the bridge in a cheerful light which didn't match the faces of the crew.

"Somebody has to say it, might as well be me," said Betty. "Are we really going to show those Censorial bastards how to get to our home?"

Roger snapped, "What's the alternative? Be captured and let them torture it out of us?"

"I don't want to be tortured. But I don't want to see Fiera covered in craters either. There's an alternative a ninety degree turn away." Betty waved at the shoal visible out her window.

"You can't be serious!" said Soon.

Betty shrugged. "I don't like it. But is it worse than the other two?"

Half the bridge crew started talking at once. Landry contemplated the suggestion. If it was just him and a willing crew he'd consider doing it if there were no better options. With his wife and child on board—no.

"There's more than those three options," he said, voice pitched loud enough to cut through the babble. "We've only explored a small fraction of this expanse. We could go into unexplored space and break contact. Or get out of sight, drop into normal space, and wait. We have the supplies for a long cruise. That warship was doing local patrols. I doubt they have food for months."

That ended the argument. Everyone looked relieved, even Betty.

"For now we'll continue down this passage. When we reach the opening it'll be decision time."

As Landry thought through the decision tree he glanced at Betty. The key factor was how soon the Censorials followed them into this passage. If Betty could detect Censorial radar before they were close enough to get a usable echo Landry could maneuver to avoid them.

No signals had been detected by the time *Azure Tarn* emerged from the shoals. That left several options open on Landry's decision tree.

"That's it, now we're totally doomed," snarled Betty.

"That's not doom. That's salvation," said Captain Landry, discarding all his plans.

Filling the sky ahead of them was a storm, writhing streamers of purple and red shot through with flickers of lightning. There was no nearby object to judge its size against but Landry suspected it was larger than the one they'd run into before.

"Roger, take us into the storm." Going straight into the open had been the worst option. Easily seen, no place to hide. But that was before he saw the storm.

By now the helmsman had given up on complaining about his orders. "Aye-aye."

After an hour of cruising Soon updated their course to adapt to the storm's observed motion. Some crew were sent below to help Marcus and Alys with securing the hold. The remaining loose cargo might not stand up to being shaken by the storm.

***

The hold was ugly. Tying down vehicles in minimum time led to expedients such as smashing windows to run a strap through the inside or pounding a staple into the roof to make an attachment point. Broken crates were stuffed in bags or wrapped in tarps.

Marcus hooked the end of a tie-down strap to one of the few exposed latches on the deck. A few twists of the ratchet pulled the strap taut, pressing a line of floaters against the deck. He stood and looked around at his helpers. They were finished securing the floaters. Now everyone was reaching under vehicles to gather up parts and debris.

"Everyone hang on, get ready to flip!" he called. Then he pulled a handcomm from his pocket. "Hold to bridge."

"Bridge, aye," came his father's voice.

"Request hold artificial gravity set to negative five percent."

"Confirm negative five percent."

"Negative five, confirmed."

"Will do."

Marcus put the handcomm away and took hold of the strap with both hands. "Everyone grab hold! We're flipping. Stay put until stuff stops falling." He felt uncomfortable shouting orders at the first mate, but she was clear that this was his project, he was in charge, and she was just a worker bee here.

Tets, Welly, and Soon he had no trouble bossing around.

Marcus wobbled as his weight dwindled away. Then his feet left the deck as the AG went from slight positive to slight negative.

As the force strengthened again he dangled from the strap, his feet toward the overhead. A glance around showed everyone else was dangling as well. Alys had cheated by getting back in the operator's cab for the crane.

The hold rang with the rings of metal pieces bouncing onto the overhead. Floaters scraped against each other as slack in tie-downs let them shift. There was a smell of dust—the hold's corners were being shaken out.

More parts fell as tilting floaters dropped anything caught on their underside. When the silence lasted five seconds Marcus let go of his strap. At five percent it wasn't much of a drop.

With his feet on the overhead he looked at his dangling helpers. "Okay. Meet up at the aft end. We're going to walk through. Alys, bags."

The fore and aft ends of the hold were packed deck to overhead with fully secured floaters. They'd barely budged with the gravity flip. That left only half the hold for them to walk.

"Is this a FOD walk?" asked Tets. Cleaning up 'Foreign Object Debris' was a routine and hated chore.

Alys passed out sturdy canvas bags to everyone.

"It's like a FOD walk," answered Marcus. "Just pick up the big stuff. The little bits we'll have to live with. We don't have time for it."

He bent over to pick up a shard of a broken window the size of his foot. "Don't bother with little crysplas fragments. We don't care if they're broken more. Just pick up debris big enough to damage something when the storm shakes us."

"How big?" asked Welly.

Right, keep it simple. "Anything bigger than the palm of your hand, bag."

"My hand or hers?" joked Tets. He high-fived Welly. His hand was almost twice as wide as hers.

"Hers. Let's go." Marcus stepped forward and scooped up a power transducer. It stuck in the middle of the bag, too light in 5% gravity to overcome friction.

The first mate picked up a shredded fender. The rest started work. The hard part was staying balanced. Bending over brought one foot off the plates. Putting it back down too hard would kick the crewman into the air.

Marcus grabbed Alys to keep her from going face-first into a pile of crysplas gravel.

"Could we have more gravity?" she asked.

He pointed at the floaters suspended overhead. "I don't want to strain the tie downs."

"Oh. Right." Alys gingerly picked up a stator.

***

Garbled reflections became clear radar pings as the Censorials emerged from the shoals. Betty couldn't find any change in their azimuth. The Censorials were headed straight for *Azure Tarn*.

"They're not being very chatty," remarked Captain Landry. "I expected regular threats, promises of mercy, and demands for cooperation whenever they had line of sight."

Roger didn't need to keep his hands on the controls now. The autopilot could keep the ship in a straight line. "Targeting radar is a threat," he said.

"True," answered the captain.

"They might have heard how our chat with the cutter went," said Betty.

The bridge was silent for a while.

Then Betty began twisting dials on her console. "Finally! They're close enough for me to pick up secondary echoes."

"Secondary?" asked Roger.

"Radar works by bouncing a radio wave off our hull. When the echo gets to their receiver they read our angle and distance. But some of the echo bounces off their hull and comes back to us. I know when the first echo bounced off us so I can measure the distance to them."

She studied a waveform on her display. "Too garbled to tell much about them. It's stronger than I expected. Not a straight sixth power return. That ship must have a flat surface facing us, maybe even corners."

"Good," said Landry. "Will it catch us before we reach the storm?"

"I need more data before I can estimate its speed."

Before she had enough data the cargo hold workers were released to their regular duties. Soon took over the calculations.

"We'll reach the center of the storm before it's in directed energy range. Not that we'll go there," said the astrogator.

"As we close on the storm we'll lose speed," said Roger. "I already backed off a hair. Aether density is going up."

Soon nodded. "I included an estimate."

"What I'm wondering," said Captain Landry, "is when the Censorials will do that math."

"Looks like they already did," answered Betty. "Check out the aft camera."

Landry pulled up the feed on his repeater screen. Six dots formed a circle around a dot that must be the mother ship in the center. "Yep, we have incoming fighters."

"What's the plan for dealing with them?" asked Roger. His voice was calm but Landry could see the tension in his hunched shoulders.

"Cube-square law," answered the captain firmly. He looked around the bridge. Most were confused. The first mate rolled her eyes at him. He turned back to Roger. "Make sure we're at max speed. Wait for Betty to complain."

That produced a snort from the sensor tech but Roger answered with a firm, "Yes, sir."

Before they needed to cut speed again the winds of the storm started shaking the ship. Not hard, just a shimmy. But it was enough to bring back memories of the storm they'd run into outbound from Fiera.

Landry and Soon studied the currents of the storm. Bands of pastel fog swirled around the center of the storm. They judged the turbulence of different streams by the mix of colors. A glow through the fog told them the core was compressed enough to release the energy of fracturing aether. Flickers showed lightning spreading out from the core.

"Okay, when we enter the purple current pull up and stick with it," ordered the captain. "That will carry us over the top fast. Might be a chance to break contact long enough to drop into normal space."

"Aye-aye," said Roger.

The six fighters were closing in on *Azure Tarn*. They began pinging with their targeting radar. The dart-shaped fighters didn't offer enough of a reflection for Betty to pick up secondary echoes. To her joy the captain finally authorized using the small antennas to ping the Censorials. They were slowing, not able to push through the thickening aether with as much authority as the larger freighter. Their formation was losing its crisp hexagonal shape as gusts shoved one or another out of position.

"There's the purple current," said Soon. She spoke out of nervousness. Everyone on the bridge saw it filling the forward window.

The ship bucked as she hit the turbulent layer between the current and surrounding maelstrom. Roger brought her back on course. Then they were immersed in purple fog. The ship swayed hard to starboard. Roger went with the turn, aligning *Azure Tarn* with the flow.

As the ride smoothed out Roger said, "We're in the middle of the current."

"Good work," said Captain Landry.

"Fighters are cutting the corner," reported Betty.

"Good. Stupid bastards don't know what they're playing with. How's their formation?"

"All over the place, sir. I think one just moved completely across the circle."

"I'll bet." Landry chuckled. "Wait until they try to take those kites through the boundary layer."

Soon ran calculations on the enemy craft. "They're falling behind. The turbulence is costing them more speed than the shorter path is saving them."

"Yep. Cube square law at work. They have more surface area per unit mass so the aether can push them around." The captain was smug enough to make the first mate roll her eyes again.

Betty cursed. "Missile launch!"

Shoulders tensed around the bridge. "Evasive action, sir?" asked Roger.

"Steady as she goes," said the captain. "Wait until they're closer."

Betty read off the range to the fast moving missiles. The captain didn't tense until they reached the current's boundary layer.

"They're losing their speed," reported Betty. "Fighters are catching up to them."

"Missiles are even lighter than fighters," said Landry. "Terrible environment for them."

"The missiles are hitting the boundary layer," said Betty. "Whoa, all over the place now. None of them made it through. A couple are headed back toward the fighters."

Now the bridge crew wore smiles. More respectful than usual glances went toward the captain. Even the first mate gave him one.

Marcus came to the bridge hatch. "Hold is secure as it's going to get, sir. Permission to take the jumpseat?"

"Granted." Landry thought the best thing would be for his son to nap in preparation for replacing someone else who had to come off-duty. But there was no way he'd sleep with this much excitement going on.

"Holy shit!" squealed Betty. "A missile just hit a fighter! Let me send another ping."

Everyone on the bridge held their breath.

"Oh my God. Yes. There's only five fighters out there. And the missiles are too far away to see."

They were too tired and stressed to cheer, but there were sighs of relief across the bridge.

Betty had more news. "Two of the fighters are going back the way they came. The others are spreading out, still heading toward us."

"Bringing the news to Momma. We'll see how well that one handles the storm," said Landry.

"I'm not sure how much longer we'll handle it," said Roger. "I've cut relative speed to zero. We're just drifting with the current. And pressure is still going up."

"The current must be going toward the core," said Landry. "We'll move outward before it gets too high."

"What happens when the mother ship comes after us?" asked Welly.

"Depends how aerodynamic it is," said the captain.

"Can't be very," said Betty. "It reflects too well."

"Which means it may be time to talk to them," said Landry. He switched his repeater to a file he'd been making notes in. "First mate, tell me what you think of this."

***

"I know how the blasted laws of physics work, Lead," snarled Captain Wing. The Fighter Operations Leader acted as if the pilot's death was Wing's fault instead of that of the blasted traitors who'd led them here.

"I apologize, sir," said the FOL. "I'm just suggesting the best use of our remaining fighters is to surround the storm and watch for the freighter to emerge."

"I'm not going to let them hide forever." Wing forced himself to stop grinding his teeth.

"Sir, incoming signal," said the communications officer.

"Put it on," said Wing. "Which fighter is it?"

"Um, not a fighter, sir."

Captain Landry's face formed on the screen, seated in his

command chair. Lane and Marcus stood stern-faced by his shoulders. "Censorial Commander, this is Captain Niko Landry of the *Azure Tarn*. I hope you're enjoying this chase. It's certainly been an adventure for us."

Landry leaned forward. "I know you've been ordered to bring us back. I assure you we have no interest in harming the Censorate. We just want to go home. If we have to we can go out of sight and drop into normal space. We can stay there for months. Can you?"

The transmission cut off.

Captain Wing suddenly felt calmer than he had in a full day. "Comm, delete that insolence from the log. Helm, take us directly to the freighter, best speed."

The senior chief on the helm said respectfully, "Sir, doctrine requires the chief engineer's approval before entering volumes with aether density over—"

"Yes, yes, ask him," interrupted Wing.

The brief conversation was followed by the chief engineer's face appearing on the captain's personal display. "Sir, if we were flying a cruiser or destroyer we could chase those traitors right into the core of the storm. *Implacable* isn't designed for that kind of stress."

Captain Wing unclenched his jaw to say, "You're saying our ship's structure is too flimsy?"

"It's not the structure, sir." The engineer's face was replaced with a rotating diagram of the carrier. It was a thick disk, one face pocked with sockets to hold the fighters. The drive unit projected from the other side, ready to accelerate *Implacable* to match her fighters' speed when bringing them back on board.

The engineer continued, "It's her shape. A flat bow gathers the aether instead of deflecting—"

"Lieutenant Commander, I did pass basic spacemanship. *Implacable* has cruised in dense aether before."

"Yessir. But the storm has gusts. One could exceed our limits."

"Fine. We'll put fighters out to warn of gusts."

A thoughtful look passed across the chief engineer's face. Then it went back to grim. "Even so, sir, I can't authorize entry to the storm."

"Very well. You're relieved."

The deputy also required relief. The third engineer approved it, after a brief chat with the helmsman directing response to gusts and severe turbulence.

Implacable headed into the storm, launching the last of her hyperspace-capable fighters.

***

"Density's going up, sir," said Roger. No one was surprised. *Azure Tarn* was shaking harder despite reducing thrust to zero.

"Time to exit this highway," said Captain Landry. "Quarter ahead thrust. Hard to starboard."

"Aye-aye." They didn't feel a change as the ship yawed to the side of the current. The boundary was a mix of green and blue, turbulence showing in the chaotic movement.

"When you reach another current follow it," said Landry gently. "Do it by feel." His voice was just audible over the roar of aether past the hull.

When the ship crossed out of the current the roar intensified. *Azure Tarn* pitched and yawed. Clots of fog flowed over the ship, obscuring the view then moving past. Lightning flashed to port. Metal groaned as the hull strained under the pressure.

A clear orange current showed, shifting to dead ahead as Roger steered toward it. More bits of fog swirled in between. The turbulence was strong. Landry considered ordering Roger to steer over it. No. He'd delegated the job, time to let Roger work. He clamped his jaw shut.

As the ship forged into the chaos she kept thrashing about. Landry realized Roger was riding the vortices, letting the ship's nose make a full circle then thrusting forward into the next swirl of aether before backing off on the engines again. *Boy knows what he's doing.*

The shaking was worse as they approached the orange current. Its boundary layer was thicker than the one they broke through to escape the purple current. There were no simple vortices now, just forces battering at the ship with no pattern.

The creaking of the hull could only be heard in the momentary lull as the aether shifted to come at them from a new direction. Then a screech of tearing metal overwhelmed the sound of the storm.

"Shit!" cried Betty. "The dish is gone!"

Welly shouted, "Hull breach! Aether is shorting out the lines. Shutting down breakers."

Roger struggled with his controls. "I lost the forward attitude thrusters!"

"I'll have to blow out the aether and reseal," said Welly, barely audible over the storm.

Landry waved her down. "Wait!" The deck was rolling too much for anyone to move safely around the ship.

"Dammit!" Roger slammed multiple levers to their limits. The hull groaned. Then the green fog over the bridge windows cleared. They were in the current. Shaking and noise died away as he jockeyed them to the center of the stream.

"Permission to execute damage control?" asked Welly, already on her feet.

"Granted," said the captain.

Marcus popped out of the jumpseat. "I can help."

"Fine. Both of you suit up."

***

Welly reached for the locker labeled 'DAMAGE CONTROL SUITS.'

"Wait," said Marcus. "Those are for vacuum. Let's use the EVA suits. They handle high pressure."

"Can we spare the time?"

"Can we afford a ripped suit?"

The bulky EVA suits had all been moved to lockers by the upper deck airlock as part of preparing the hold for the floaters. They helped each other don them. That involved more bracing against the ship's lurches than holding gear.

When Welly's helmet snapped into place Marcus began inspecting her seals. She confined her complaint to tapping a toe in frustration. Her return inspection was cursory.

Then they headed down the forward stairs. The landing had two hatches labeled 'CARGO HOLD' and 'ELECTRONICS BAY.' Welly yanked the latter open.

"Crap," she said.

Bits of orange mist were visible in the accessway. Some clung to the deck or bulkhead.

"We can contain it." Marcus turned to the environmental panel for the stairwell. He increased the pressure setting to 1.3 atmospheres. Air began blowing through the open hatch, sending the mists into circular flurries.

"Come on." Welly waved him through then closed the hatch behind him.

He took patches out of the DC locker while Welly went from one access panel to another, peeking in to assess the damage. The 'MAIN DISH PWR CNDT' panel puffed out orange mist.

"That's it. Six inch round."

Marcus handed her the patch.

"Four by two. Vacctape. Clamp ring, four inch." He kept passing Welly the necessary supplies. She had all the tools for the job on her belt.

"There, one hole done." Welly moved to the next panel. "Oh, this isn't bad. Two inch round." All the tears in the hull were places where the sensor dish had been firmly attached before tearing loose. She efficiently sealed them all.

"Done. Done with the holes. We still need to get rid of the aether." She waved at a clump floating past her face, then rubbed her hand on the bulkhead to scrape off the sticky vapor.

Marcus said, "Usually we'd jump to normal space and dump the compartment to vacuum. But God help us if the Censorials follow us through before we're done."

"Yeah. And jumping back into a moving storm could kill us. We could pump the compartment down to vacuum but the seals won't hold against the pressure difference." Welly turned in place to survey the compartment as she thought. "Ah. Marcus, start pumping air out of the compartment."

"Okay." He reset the environmental controls. Even through the suit helmets they could hear the whine of the pump as it forced air out through the hull valve. The orange mist drifted toward the intake.

"And now to solve the pressure problem." Welly opened the hatch. It slammed against the stops, flung hard by the 1.3 overpressure in the stairwell.

They could see the higher pressure air rush in by the way it forced the mist ahead of it. Much of the aether went straight into the pump intake.

"That's working. Clean up next," said Welly. The EVA suits had an external line for the air tank. It was intended to supply another suit. She opened the access panel closest to the hatch and blasted it with air from the line. Bits of orange vapor flew out and were carried into the current toward the pump. When they were all gone she moved on to the next panel.

Marcus used his air line on the bits of aether clinging to the bulkhead and deck. "Why the hell is this stuff so damn sticky."

"Surface tension. It's a pure fluid. No atoms."

"I hate hyperspace physics."

When all the aether had been blown out Welly inspected the power lines to the attitude thrusters. "Looks clean now." She called the bridge to request a breaker reset. The indicator lights came on.

Roger tested the thrusters and declared them functional.

"Thank God," said Welly. "Now we can get out of these damn suits."

"Hold off on that. I want to talk to the captain first."

Eying someone suspiciously in a spacesuit required turning the entire body to face him. Welly shuffled her feet around to do so. "What?"

"We set the air in here to 1.3 atmospheres to hold the seals in place. What if we did that to the whole ship?"

"We explode when we go back to normal space."

"Yeah, we'd have to reduce pressure before we transition."

"It would counter the external pressure. Hmmm." Welly thought a moment. "We'd have to wear suits. Should be doing that anyway in case the hull breaches. Let's talk to the captain."

***

Captain Landry interrupted Marcus halfway through his description of his idea. "Let me get Gander on the line."

Once the intercom was open Marcus started through it again.

When he finished, Landry said, "What do you think, Chief?"

"It'll work. Need to go back down to one atmosphere before we go back to normal space. Want to close the interior hatches to compartmentalize breaches. There's a lot of reserve air. Might as well use it all."

"Then we'll do it once everyone is suited up. Betty, are those fighters still hanging around?"

"Still pinging us every two minutes. Haven't missed one yet," she reported.

"Are they keeping close to us?"

"No, the storm is blowing them all over the sky. Still in radar range."

"Then we can ignore them for a bit. Go suit up. Roger, let Marcus take the helm. You and Soon suit up too."

"Find where Alys is hiding while you're at it," said Marcus. He had to adjust the helm chair, lowering the seat and spreading out the arms so he could fit in it wearing the EVA suit.

Putting everyone in suits wasn't the most time consuming part of the operation. Gander put everyone who could be spared to opening hatches and access panels. He didn't trust the air circulation system to handle a pressure surge that large.

Once every door on Gander's list was open the chief engineer opened up the ship's nitrogen and oxygen tanks. *Azure Tarn's* designers prepared for a hull breach that left the whole ship in vacuum. The interior pressure was just over two atmospheres when the tanks were empty.

Then Gander insisted on closing all the doors again.

The first mate led Marcus, Welly, and Soon back onto the bridge. As Marcus fastened the seat belt on the jumpseat he asked, "Did we miss any excitement?"

"No," answered the captain. "We're following the same current. It's heading into the heart of the storm. We'll have to get out soon. Those damn fighters are still watching us so we can't go back to normal space."

"What if we transition to normal space and wait for them to go away?" asked Welly.

Captain Landry shook his head. "If we sit there until the storm moves past the mother ship can come through. We need to break contact before hiding."

"Pressure gradient is increasing," said Roger.

"Very well. Take us out of the current."

Roger pivoted *Azure Tarn* away from the center of the storm. He cut speed as she reached the boundary of the current. The exit was smoother than the last time. The hull made a few faint creaks, nothing like the groans they'd heard before.

Landry pivoted to face Marcus and gave him an approving nod.

The turbulence shook the ship about as badly as before. Roger rode with the vortices. Their course was a random walk through the storm. Soon had declared this was as likely to find a favorable current as a more deliberate search pattern.

"Found a current," said Roger. He fought the ship toward the pink streak.

"Don't," said Soon. "It's headed straight into the core."

With a curse the helmsman twisted the ship away. Vortices tossed her about. They worked toward the edges of the storm.

"There's a current above us," said Welly, leaning to look out her window.

Roger pitched the ship up to get a look at it.

"That'll take us straight toward the fighters," warned Betty.

"Do it," said the captain. "If we move fast enough we might go past and lose them."

The green current was weaker than the others they'd been in. The boundary layer shook the ship without straining the hull. Once in the center of the current Roger increased thrust to move faster than the flow.

"We're closing on the fighters," said Betty.

"Are they reacting to us?" asked the captain.

"Can't tell. The storm's been bouncing them around like crazy."

"Acknowledged."

Betty smiled. "This is a reaction. They just increased their ping rate. Every ten seconds."

The fighters were still caught in the maelstrom as *Azure Tarn* rode the current past them. The frantic pinging continued as they fell further behind.

"If we break contact we can drop to normal space," said Captain Landry.

"Still getting echoes off us," reported Betty. "But fading."

Landry pressed the intercom switch. "Gander, how long would it take to pump the air back down to normal?"

"Twenty minutes at least," said the chief engineer. "Pumping up high pressure tanks is harder than letting them bleed off."

"Right. We'll have to be sure we've broken contact then."

Betty shouted, "Low frequency ping! The mother ship saw us!"

The green current curved around high pressure regions. *Azure Tarn* went around a bend into a straightaway. Filling the far end was the Censorial ship. The boundary of the current bulged out as it flowed around the huge vessel.

A line of aether reaching halfway between them turned white then spread out, fading into the rest of the current.

"At least we're out of energy weapon range," said Landry. "Take us into the turbulence."

Roger turned hard to port.

***

"Aether's too thick to hit her at this range," said the gunner's mate.

"Acknowledged," said Captain Wing. "Fire as we close."

His crew had lost their frustration. With prey in sight they all focused on the hunt.

The sensor tech announced, "Target evading plus-Y."

"Stand by," said the astrogator. It took him less than half a minute to calculate three courses. "Best closing time is to stay in the current until we halve the distance, then go direct."

"Stay in current, aye," said the helmsman. *Implacable* proceeded forward.

Captain Wing let a smile escape. He'd weeded his crew down to the ones he needed. No more requesting permission or orders for every action. They knew what to do and they did it.

The bridge elevator doors hissed open. Wing turned to see three officers step onto the bridge.

"Come to see the finish, doctor?" he asked his chief medical officer.

The doctor shrugged.

Wing turned to the former XO and chief engineer. "Gentlemen, you were confined to quarters."

The doctor found his voice. "Sir, I must evaluate your fitness to retain command. Will you accompany me to sickbay?"

Wing's face froze. His whole body turned cold in outrage. "I will not. We are engaged in combat."

The last word was underscored by the slap of superheated aether striking the hull. "Almost," said the gunner's mate.

The doctor stood stiffly at attention. "By doctrine I must consult with the acting executive officer."

"Very well." Wing waved the Fighter Operations Leader over. "Lead, once you've reassured the doctor about his anxieties, please see those two to the brig, since their quarters can't hold them."

Then Wing turned and walked to the center of the bridge. He didn't want to listen to mutinous talk. If the FOL could settle it before anyone needed to be court-martialed, good.

"Shift to direct course," called the astrogator.

"Forty degrees to starboard, aye," said the helmsman.

The viewscreen now showed the churning vortices of the maelstrom in place of the smooth green of the current. *Implacable* lurched as she felt the turbulence.

Wing glanced back. The XO and chief engineer were now whispering to the FOL. Well, if they wanted to be spaced for attempted mutiny he wouldn't stop them.

The astrogator ordered, "Six degrees pitch up, four degrees port." The helmsman echoed the numbers back as he adjusted course.

"We're closing on the traitors," said the sensor tech. The excitement in his voice was contagious.

"Hull stress is up but still within limits," said the damage control officer.

"Acknowledged," said Captain Wing. "Continue pursuit."

***

Azure Tarn shook like a chew toy in a puppy's mouth as she plunged through the storm. The bridge crew had all seat-belted and even put on their seldom-used shoulder straps. Even secured to his chair Landry felt aches from the shaking. His neck hurt worst, the muscles sore from trying to hold his head steady against the lurches and rolls.

"It's out of the current and closing!" yelled Betty over the storm's roar.

Roger fought the vortices to steer as straight away from the Censorial ship as they could. He wound up tacking back and forth across the desired path, sometimes intentionally using gusts to get extra distance, more often blown off course by an unexpected surge of aether.

"Damn, it's coming straight at us," shouted Betty. "How come it isn't being pushed around?"

"Cube-square," said the captain. "It has too much mass to care."

A line of text from the first mate appeared on his repeater. "Your speech may have pissed them off too much."

He typed in return, "Yeah. I wanted to lull him into not taking risks. Guess it backfired."

"Good try though," she replied.

The aether around them glowed with light as the Censorials fired again. Landry held his hand over his face to block the glare. This time there was a crack-whoosh sound as the light faded. A flicker of lightning ahead of them was pale in comparison.

"No electrical damage," declared Welly. "Structure holding. Oh, we lost the galley windows."

"Acknowledged," shouted Landry. By themselves not important damage, but it was an opening for the storm to tear at the ship. Worse, it meant the Censorial ship was close enough to score real hits. They may have only survived because the aether was thick enough to dissipate the bolt. If they entered a patch of thin aether . . .

Captain Landry ordered, "Roger, take us into the densest aether you can find."

"Aye-aye," said the helmsman.

Landry gripped his chair. He'd rather the storm killed them than the Censorials.

***

"Atmosphere venting from the target," reported the sensor tech. "Definite hull breach."

Captain Wing slapped the gunner's mate on the shoulder. "Well done, Guns, well done. Now belay firing until you're close enough to target their drive. We need prisoners. I want to immobilize her then take her under tow."

At the last words the helmsman flashed an astonished glance at the captain, then changed his expression back to professionally calm.

The junior officers manning stations on the bridge traded looks. The astrogator spoke up. "Sir, towing under these conditions will be difficult."

Wing's tone was unconcerned. "Yes, we'll have to wait for the storm to pass."

"Airlock six lost outer door. Team en route to reinforce inner door," said the damage control officer.

"Very well," said Wing. "How's the structure reading?"

"Currently all within limits, sir. A few places have gone over limit but no cracks yet." The DCO swallowed before continuing. "We'll need a full tear-down to inspect for damage when we return to port, sir."

"We'll all deserve a good long shore leave after we drag these traitors home for trial."

Wing glanced over at the knot of quietly arguing senior officers. Were they still going on? Well, there was one way to settle that. He summoned the ship's master at arms to the bridge. He could take the XO and chief engineer to the brig, where they'd stop distracting the doctor from his duties.

"Target's engines locked in," said the gunner's mate. "And . . . damn."

"Problem, Guns?" asked the captain.

"Density's too damn high, sir. If I fire now the shock wave will wreck the emitter."

"Very well. Stay on her. Fire as soon as it's safe."

"Aye-aye."

The helmsman asked, "Sir, how close do you want to get to that ship? She's blowing around like a leaf. I'd hate to ram her—by accident."

"Hmmm." Wing studied *Azure Tarn's* movement in the display. "No closer than five hundred meters."

"Aye-aye."

"Sir, do you have a moment?" called the Fighter Operations Leader.

Wing walked over to the group. "Yes, what is it?"

"Sir, as acting executive officer, I request that you take *Implacable* out of this storm."

A lurch sent the doctor sprawling across a console. The other officers side-stepped to keep their balance. Wing merely flexed his knees to absorb the shock.

"Now?" Wing demanded. He pointed at the main display. "We've caught them. A bit of thin aether and we can cripple their ship. We've won. And you want to throw it away, let them spread their poison elsewhere?"

The FOL set his jaw. "Sir, the ship is in danger. She's not built for these conditions."

"No. That's final. If you repeat the request you'll be relieved."

The bridge elevator opened. The master at arms and two of his deputies stepped out.

The FOL turned to the doctor. "I find the captain is recklessly endangering the ship and crew."

The chief medical officer declared, "Then I find Captain Wing unfit for command. Sir, please report to sickbay."

Implacable pitched under a gust. The XO held the doctor on his feet.

"I'll be smashed if I will," snarled Wing. "This is mutiny!"

"No, sir. This is my duty," said the doctor calmly.

Wing cursed. Then he turned to the master at arms. "These men are under arrest. Throw them in the brig!"

The doctor followed that by saying, "The captain is unfit for duty. Please escort him to sickbay."

The master at arms looked over the officers. He saw the XO, FOL, and chief engineer standing with the doctor. Then he said to the captain, "I'm sorry, sir. Doctrine requires me to obey the chief medical officer in these situations. Please come with me."

Wing cursed.

"Breach in fighter sockets six and fourteen!" cried the damage control officer. "Aether in the power and control lines. Radial ribs fracturing!"

"Too late," said the chief engineer.

***

The Censorial ship couldn't fit into the aft camera's field of view any more. Combined with *Azure Tarn's* thrashing about it was hard to get a good look at their pursuer. Landry just knew that it was big and close.

If he wanted an exact distance he could ask Betty. She was pinging the damn thing. She'd stopped reporting the range when it went under ten klicks. It was a lot closer now.

"Why don't they shoot and get it over with?" burst out Soon.

"Prisoners," answered Marcus. "They want to interrogate us."

Roger cursed as a violet vortex spun the ship around. For a moment they could see the grim disk of the Censorial ship in the bridge windows. Then he forced *Azure Tarn* into a blue whirlpool and they shot away again.

"What the hell? They can't be launching fighters here," said Betty as she studied the radar returns.

Landry looked at the aft camera. He froze the feed as it swept across the Censorial. "That looks more like debris than fighters."

Fighters wouldn't survive this part of the storm anyway. The two trailing *Azure Tarn* had fallen out of sight as the ship fled into the denser maelstrom.

"Yep, shedding debris," agreed Betty. "I'm receiving stronger returns on the mother ship. Must be losing hull panels, exposing interior corners."

Everyone stayed tense. They'd had hope of escape before. They kept superstitiously quiet rather than ruin their hope by speaking it aloud.

"The debris isn't dense," said Betty. "It's spreading fast, going at the speed of the gusts."

Welly said, "I see some. It's blowing like confetti."

A hull panel twenty meters across flew past the starboard side of the ship.

"Damn, that could have cut us in half," said Welly.

Landry pounded the intercom switch. "Gander, emergency transition now. Repeat, emergency transition now."

The glow in the windows faded to black. Distant stars speckled the field. *Azure Tarn* settled into normal space as if she were bolted to bedrock.

Landry took a deep breath and let it out. No vertigo. Wait. He did feel some vertigo, but compared to the abuse of the storm it was nothing.

Something on the ship went whang-whoosh. Then there was a high pitched whistle.

"That was the forward corridor hatch to the galley failing," said Welly. "And the leading edge on the port quarter is leaking air."

The intercom crackled. "I'm pumping down air as fast as I can," said Gander. "We're losing a lot so don't waste any. Going to have to do repairs in vacuum."

"Any sign of that warship?" demanded Landry.

Betty said, "Pinging in all directions. There's nothing out there."

After ten minutes of pinging the consensus was that the Censorial ship must have broken up before it could transition.

Given the option Landry would have ordered sleep all around but they couldn't do that when the access to crew quarters was in vacuum. He did let the crew nap in their suits while waiting for the air to be evacuated.

Even the bridge had to be pumped down to vacuum. It had a simple hatch to the forward corridor, not an airlock.

The corridor didn't have any noticeable damage. When Marcus and Welly led the rest into the galley they saw a disaster.

Normally the most home-like part of the ship, it had been stripped of everything loose or light. Half the furniture was gone, popped free of the deck tracks it clipped into.

Lane inspected the cabinets. "Most of the dishes are here. Plates cabinet came open, they're gone. Oh. Spice cabinet failed too. No salt or anything left."

That produced a mass groan over the suit radios.

Alys poked at a blistered patch of paint. "What did that?" she asked.

"Aether," answered Welly. "In normal space some disperses into vacuum, some sticks and sublimates into heat."

The galley dome windows were gone. Even part of the frame was torn away. Gander set Tets to cutting patches to fit over the holes.

Marcus and Welly drew the outside work. Finding the cracks in the outer hull was the hard part. One rupture was on the belly, where ramming the navigation buoys had damaged the hull. Once each was identified welding a strip of metal over it was easy.

As easy as working with hot metal in free fall can be.

It took nine hours to make *Azure Tarn* air tight again. When the last leak had been found and sealed Captain Landry gathered them in the galley.

"We're going to stand down for twenty-four hours. Get some sleep. Have a bath—no water limit. Have those shakes you've been putting off. Then we'll resume normal running. Full inspections. Catch up on maintenance. I want to wait at least a week for the storm to go by. Then we head home."

The word 'home' produced wistful looks. They were all ready to be home again. But the thought of a rest was more immediately appealing.

***

Azure Tarn reentered hyperspace to find herself in the tail end of the storm. A gentle current tried to shift the ship's bow but Roger held her steady with a flick of his fingers.

"Not picking up any signals," said Betty. "Just background noise."

"Good," said Landry. "Soon, we'll head out when you have a course for us."

Betty said, "Some of the debris from that Censorial might be valuable. Can I ping for it?"

"Absolutely not. If there's any Censorials looking for that ship they'd be on us like flies."

"Yes, sir." Her disappointment was audible.

Soon was comparing photos from the trip out to the current view. When she made a match she called out vectors to Roger. He put the ship in motion.

The storm had carried them two days travel away from the entrance to the Fieran Bubble. It took over eight days to arrive.

"Nice to see it's still there," said Roger as the entered the tunnel into the Bubble. Some chuckles from the other bridge crew said they'd shared his worry of returning to find the way home closed off forever.

"Betty, measure the tunnel, would you?" asked Captain Landry.

"Yessir." She had to power up the radar transmitters first. Once she'd integrated the results, Betty said, "Noticeably wider than when we first went through."

"Thank you." Landry sat back. It looked like Fiera would stay connected to the wider galaxy whether it liked it or not.

Once through the tunnel astrogation was easy. The shoals around Fiera's sun were stable and well mapped. In only a couple days' travel they dropped into normal space over Fiera.

Landry's heart leaped to see his homeworld again. The tan deserts and jade forests peeked out through the clouds. The traffic display showed the usual tangle of ships and stations orbiting the world. A massive containership went past them, probably headed for Svalbard with a load of textiles and medicines to exchange for refined metals and fish delicacies.

"We're cleared to land at Baslim Base," said the first mate. "Direct descent authorized. The news channels are jumping. The tariff renewal debate is now an argument over the Concord as a whole. Mardam and Lunto pulled their ships out of the Concord fleet and are threatening to form a new arrangement with Svalbard and Iolite."

"Oh, God, not another war," said Welly. "My mother told me about living through the last one."

"We don't need to deal with that and the Censorials," agreed Soon.

Landry chuckled. "I think the Censorate will help them all remember how much they have in common. First mate, can you get me a link to our contract officer?"

"On it," said Lane.

The face of a middle-aged naval officer appeared on Landry's repeater. His thick neck and thin stack of ribbons told of a career spent in unexciting desk jobs. "Captain JG Carmichael, Survey Office, how may I help you?"

"Hello, Carmichael, it's Niko Landry. How are you today?"

"Niko! I'm fine, thanks. Look, Niko, I can't make an interim payment on the survey contract. It's all or nothing."

"Don't worry, I'm not asking for a payment. I'm in breach anyway."

The officer's eyebrows rose. "Lane? Are you there?"

She leaned into the camera's view. "Hi, Glenn."

"Could you check Niko for fever? He just said he doesn't want money."

Lane laughed. "I think we're good on that. We have bigger worries now."

"What kind of worries?" asked Carmichael.

"Worries for you, too," said Landry. "I don't want to discuss it on an open line. Can I come to your office? I can be there in three hours."

"That's quitting time. But okay. If I'm not worried by your stuff you owe me dinner."

"It's a bet. Can you have your chain of command there?"

Carmichael laughed. "How much of my chain?"

"All the way to the Planetary Liaison if you can get her."

That didn't amuse him. "If you knew anything about what's going on now you'd know the Liaison is too busy for anything else. And I like you but I'll be damned if I'll put my career on the line for you until you show me something solid."

Landry nodded. "I respect that. I'll see you in three hours. Think about where you want to have dinner."

***

Censorial Commodores weren't supposed to go out in hyperspace in just a pressure suit. But the rescue specialists had been worked to exhaustion in hopes of finding survivors. The regular crew filling in for them were tired to the point of being accident prone. Now the staff officers were out helping recover debris and bodies. That left no one to tell Commodore Meckler to stay on his flag bridge and supervise.

As he pushed out the airlock Meckler paused to listen to his suit. No hiss of escaping air. No bubbling of hyperspace aether forcing its way in. He was secure for now.

The wait let him drink in the sight of the Phoenix Void. Wisps of purple fog obscured the glowing shoals marking where stars rested in normal space. On the far side, blurred by distant aether, an orange shoal made a wall across the sky.

The phoenix formation that gave the void its name wasn't visible on this side of the ship. But Meckler had seen it from the flag bridge. He was tired of watching. He wanted to do something.

"Please grab hold, sir," said the chief walker's mate on the suit to suit radio. The NCO operated a sleigh, a thruster built into an open frame. The other spacers coming on shift for salvage work were already holding on.

Meckler found a handhold. The chief activated the thruster, towing them all to the nearest bit of wreckage.

At fifty meters across this was the biggest piece of CNS *Implacable* they'd found yet. The first team had already made a check for survivors. Now the power supplies must be stripped out so it could safely be taken in tow.

A mild current in the aether pulled the sleigh off course before the chief could correct it. That took them around the side of the wreckage, revealing torn open compartments. Sparks jumped through the aether between torn cables.

"Everyone stay clear of the live lines," transmitted the chief. "We need to find the power sources and take them off line."

The sleigh moved to the far side. A clamp latched onto a protruding girder. Commodore Meckler eyed the jagged edges of the torn bulkheads. The injury reports he'd been reading suddenly seemed low.

"Stay in pairs," said the chief. Meckler noticed the chief didn't apply that to himself . . . or to the commodore, who found two spacers following him around.

Felt like a nasty trick to play on the kids. Those two were so green they'd be intimidated by any officer, even an ensign. Dealing with the highest ranking officer for at least ten light years in any direction left them mumbling every word except "Sir!"

Maybe the Chief did it to make Meckler be more cautious out of sympathy for the kids. Too bad.

Meckler led the way down the passageway. He tapped his voltmeter on every panel, wire, outlet, and suspicious piece of debris. Nothing.

A rupture had twisted the wreckage enough that the deck, bulkheads, and overhead all had cracks big enough to swallow a foot. A broken pipe supported a wiggling bubble of water. Broken wires waved in the aether current.

He ran the voltmeter around the edges. A cable spat sparks as he came close. "Paydirt," Meckler muttered.

The cables ran through a conduit for safety. The conduit was now ruptured, making it easy to recheck the voltage as they followed it down the passageway.

The conduit went through the bulkhead next to a hatch marked 'EMRG BTTY CMPT—High Voltage Certified Personnel Only.' The voltmeter declared the hatch was safe. It was buckled, with enough space between it and the coaming to grab it with both hands. It didn't bulge at Meckler's tug.

"Get this open," he ordered.

The spacers wrapped an insulating blanket around a prybar. They shoved it into the gap and braced their feet against the opposite bulkhead. The first few heaves did nothing. Then the hatch flew open. A wave of aether shoved Meckler hard enough to lose his grip on the bulkhead.

"Falling rocks!" spat a spacer.

The commodore pushed off toward the hatch. When he reached it he saw the reason for the swearing. A body floated in the battery compartment, dressed only in a utility uniform. The face was frozen in twisted agony.

"Poor bastard," said Meckler. "A lungful of aether hurts."

"Sir, why didn't he have a suit on?" asked a spacer.

"Because they were chasing a freighter, not whatever did *this*." Meckler waved an arm to take in the destruction of *Implacable. And because their commodore thought sending one ship was sufficient*, he reproached himself.

One of the spacers produced a black bag. The two of them fumbled fitting the corpse into it. Meckler finally helped hold the bag open.

When the bag was zipped shut, one spacer asked, "Sir, are we going to punish the people who did this?"

"Oh, yes. We're going to find the traitors. We're going to make them pay. And we're going to make their whole bleeding planet pay."

Other Works by Karl K. Gallagher

Science fiction fans, check out <u>Torchship</u>, a working-class hard SF adventure.

A captain who'll take any job if there's enough money in it. A pilot with an agenda of her own. And a mechanic with an eye on the pilot.

The crew of the Fives Full are just trying to make enough money to keep themselves in the black while avoiding the attention of a government so paranoid it's repealed Moore's Law. They're not looking for adventure in the stars . . . but they're not going to back down just because something got in their way.

The Torchship trilogy was a finalist for the 2018 Prometheus Award for best libertarian science fiction novel.

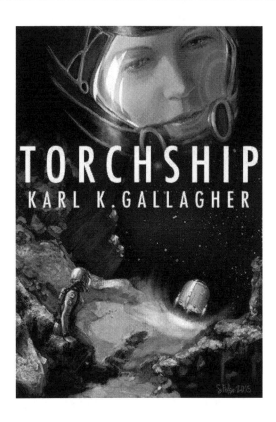

The sequels Torchship Pilot and Torchship Captain are included in the Torchship Trilogy omnibus.

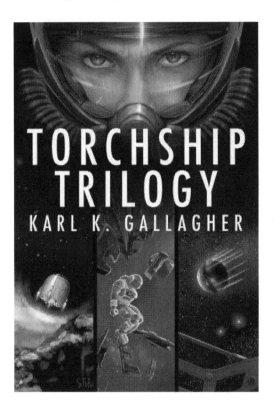

Adventure story fans will enjoy <u>The Lost War</u>:

It was supposed to be a weekend of costumed fun. Instead these medieval historical reenactors are flung into a wilderness by magic they don't understand. They must struggle to survive and deal with monsters who consider them prey . . . or worse.

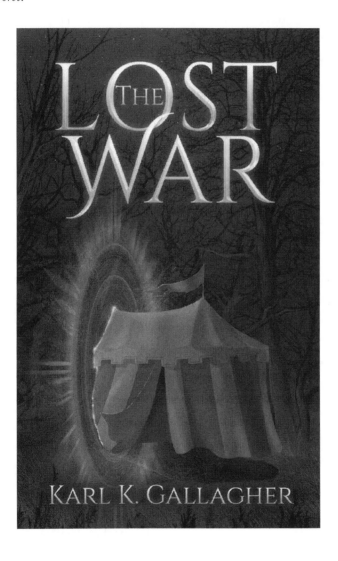

About the Author

Karl Gallagher has earned engineering degrees from MIT and USC, controlled weather satellites for the Air Force, designed weather satellites for TRW, designed a rocketship for a start-up, and done systems engineering for a fighter plane. He is husband to Laura and father to Maggie, James, and dearly missed Alanna.

About Kelt Haven Press

Kelt Haven Press is releasing print, ebook, and audiobooks by Karl K. Gallagher. For updates see:

www.kelthavenpress.com

Subscribe to the newsletter for updates on new releases.